THERE'S A TALE
IN BETWEEN

Felix,

Thank you so much

for your support bro!

Enjoy Reading!

Thank you so much

THERE'S A TALE IN BETWEEN

ADAM BASMA

NEW DEGREE PRESS

THERE'S A TALE IN BETWEEN

ISBN   978-1-63730-638-3 *Paperback*

978-1-63730-722-9 *Kindle Ebook*

978-1-63730-913-1 *Ebook*

I would like to dedicate this book to my younger self—a writer who failed to realize the possibilities are endless. You finally did it, buddy.

Contents

Author's Note

———

Piles of lined sheets of paper lie dormant in my mother's file cabinet beside her room—the remnants of stories I had written as a child, messy handwriting showing a decent plot but an all-too-lazy execution, nonetheless. Cramped hands grew weary faster than I could get out all the ideas I wanted. At twelve years old, my lack of diligence with writing subsided, and my stories remained as nothing more than pastimes at a young age when I would scribble for a while before turning the lights out and going off to bed. Whether the depth of my stories started rich or bland, the passion for putting words on the page was always there.

At the age of fourteen I began to take writing more seriously. I messed around with form and prose, turning ideas about social justice into powerful spoken word poems. I would go on to present in front of my school in seventh grade and onward, realizing the power of what one minute's worth of words could do to an audience. When I reached my senior year in high school, I was given the opportunity to write a novel for my final project.

What began as an ambitious chance to bridge the gap between my spoken word poems and a full-blown novel ended in a mediocre manuscript that I wasn't fully proud of by the end of my time.

As I now write this note, the ideas have been expanded, the experiences have been seasoned, and I have come back to this piece with a more well-rounded take on the ideas I explore in this book. I haven't had the experiences that I detail between these pages, but through lessons I have learned from peers and mentors, I've written a work of fiction that seeks to open a new door for the reader. The characters in this book are realistic, and the lives they lead have substance. They are there to challenge you as the reader to choose who you wish to feel for and to see where your morals fall.

I decided to write about this because I feel that all readers can genuinely connect to a story about family and learning the value of time as it presents itself in front of you. The characters in this book represent all of us, all that we carry through our lives, and all that gets added on. We start as a blank canvas—knowing and feeling nothing—and by the end of our lives we have so many memories to share, decisions to live with, and aspirations we couldn't live out. Through this book I wish to help readers make sense of the complications in their lives and bring a simplicity to all that we "carry" so as to help us keep on keeping on.

Additionally, this book seeks to engage readers in thinking about empathy and understanding through the eyes of the characters. Passing off people in the world who are going through rough times is all too easy. When our protagonist is plunged into an unwary situation with people he never would have surrounded himself with otherwise, he is pushed to engage with them rather than pass them off. He is challenged to work with them rather than try to get around them. All together the story details a life-changing section of someone's life and how the importance of just one journey for closure can send someone through more than they ever imagined.

To feel is to express internal gratitude for a piece of art that is presented before a reader. The power that words have—whether up on a stage or on the comfiest couch in your house or in the window nook where you never cease to read—words can have power. The power of this book will hopefully reach readers of all ages, backgrounds, and religions. Spirituality and hope for the afterlife are themes throughout this book. We carry so many decisions and the weight of our actions throughout the entirety of our life, all while thinking how or if they will affect what happens to us when we die. In understanding that these are anxieties we all have, I am hopeful that readers will use this piece to feel more connected to those beside them or those they meet for the first time.

When I was a child, I wrote as I do now. I was seeking to make someone feel something genuine in my writing. Now that I have grown older, I look to that same end; however, the ideas I can generate are backed by true knowledge and maturity rather than youthful ignorance. Bliss does not always come from what we don't know, and reading can help us make sense of things we have experienced or will in the future. Either way, we can only grow further.

At twenty-one years old, I seek to write a culmination of the things I know and the things I think I know between these pages, married like lessons and told like stories by fires that couldn't rage long enough to withstand their length. Through this piece of writing a young boy seeks to pursue his ultimate dream—to make sense of all those lined sheets of paper sitting in his mother's file cabinet. To make sense of all the loss and fear and happiness he has felt ever since. To make sense of all life's wonders, here on earth, and what we perceive once we pass on. To understand one another rather than judging someone's character based on a section of their life. A young boy is still raging through the passion of the book, but hopefully a more mature and educated one can take his place to tell this story. From sheets of lined paper to the keys of a computer and now to a book, I present to you a story about family, grief, and the world we seek to make sense of each and every day.

Chapter 1

——

The most important things I know about life, I learned through death. My grandparents were hoarders—not to the extent that we couldn't see their floor, or that they had mounds of garbage in their living room, but they were hoarders. The closets were filled floor to ceiling with newspapers, there was always something to move out of the way, and there always seemed to be a mess. When you cleaned the mess, there was another mess, and another took its place until there wasn't anything else to do except just leave it as it was.

I think that's how it was for my grandmother in her final years. The whites from her smile slowly shrunk between her lips. Her upbeat pace and laughter were exchanged for a cough and sorrowful eyes. Inevitably, life nearing its end weighs heavily on all our souls, I believe. When I got the news that she had passed away, my family and I rushed down to their home that night. The hoarding had gotten worse than ever before.

My grandfather was sitting in the living room with boxes of old photos dumped around him, scattered across the floor like a puddle of memories aged older than himself. When I bent to hug him, his breath was as calm as a wading sea, his hands as warm as summer air. "Hey there, Alec," he said, his tone soft and calm. I wondered why he wasn't crying, why he wasn't in the room with Grandma. My mother went in first. I took a walk around the house, gazing at the pictures on the walls as I awaited my turn.

Tiptoeing through the halls I found boxes opened by a single flap exposing their contents, everything from dusty board games to decades old knickknacks. It was the first time I didn't smell my grandmother's aromatically familiar lemon magic cake wisping through the air and landing right beneath my nose. The first time I wasn't met by her "hello!" triggered by the sound of me barreling through the door and running to have her clutch me in her soft arms. I was much younger then. At eighteen years old I had been to my grandparents' house only half a dozen times—probably why each was so memorable to me.

I was starting to see why my parents didn't want us experiencing that. The bedrooms were worse than anywhere else in the house. Piles and piles of old clothes, sports equipment, and shoes overtook an entire room. In the other I found war memorabilia that my grandfather had kept alongside overflowing boxes of digitized photos they had taken before I was born. It wasn't rancid, but the smell was stale, musty almost. The cold didn't lend any benefit, and the atmosphere was unforgiving and dark. I could only catch a glimpse of each room from the door frame as the aged hinges were loud enough to startle my grandfather and expose my nosiness.

My mother called me from the other room, and I went on back to the living room. It was my turn. I hadn't ever seen a dead person before in my life. I was only eighteen, and death was just something caused by the right button in a video game or the play button of a movie. I stepped in expecting to be shocked by the horror you see from a scary movie or a ghost shuddering before my eyes. Instead, what I saw changed my perspective forever.

The room was pristine. Not a single item was out of place. No old board games lying around, no trash in the wastebaskets—everything was where it needed to be. I was taken aback by the cleanliness of the room. For the first time in my life, I saw my grandmother without mess. For the first time I saw her without stress, without a forced smile. She wasn't struggling to get up from the arm of the chair on both forearms just to expend all her energy for the remote across the room. She wasn't crying in pain. She wasn't arguing with my grandfather.

So, sitting here now a week later, in the back of the funeral parlor looking at her casket, I needed to ask my grandfather why that was.

I waited until he rose from his chair and followed him outside. He sat down on the bench, pulling a flask out from his coat pocket. I could see his sigh in the light of the streetlamp complemented by the crisp winter air.

Sitting next to him, I gave him a minute to recognize my presence. I felt a sorrow for my grandmother in this moment. I hadn't taken enough time to sit with her to chat about things. Things beyond my schoolwork, friends, and basic life events.

I didn't ask her how she felt growing up, where she learned some of her greatest lessons, what she loved to do as a kid. I felt bad for thinking about prying on the subject of hoarding and was preparing to leave when he spoke up.

"Whatever it is you want to ask, please do it. This silence is much worse than anything you'd have to say, believe me," he said before pressing the flask to his lips.

I took a second to go over my wording, fumbling over the first words trying not to be too blunt.

"Grandma's room. Why was it so much different than the rest of the house? Not just clean, but the whole ambiance; it was like a whole other universe compared to the rest of your house," I asked.

"Boy, when you grow old, you'll see how life gets you. I know you kids weren't allowed over to our house a lot," he replied.

He was right. Either we went there for an emergency or when my parents were running late from work. They only lived a few minutes away on a much busier street of our town, yet we rarely saw the inside of their house. They were always with us, though. Always at family parties, always at celebrations; they were always just there. Grandpa never smiled but he was never upset either, just taking it all in. Growing up I figured that's just always how it was.

"We're all hoarders, Alec. Whether it's in here," he said, pointing to his head, "or in your home. Wherever it may be, we all just can't let go, not at my age especially."

I looked into the street gazing forward. I didn't know what to say. If I had embarrassed or offended him, I really hadn't meant to.

"Alec, we live on that busy street. Cars race up and down doing their thing—racing to work, racing to commit a crime, racing to live, and racing to die. Everyone is holding so many things inside of them and racing to solve them. It gets to a point where you can't solve everything, and you end up like a clogged sink, filling up. It never stops until it spills, and when it's done ruining your floors it seeps through the ground below you, exposing you to other people. Through your years it never stops, and then there it is. Inside where your grandmother is, all the people around her here today, there it is," he said.

"I—I don't know what to say Grandpa. I'm sorry," I continued until he replied.

"That's all right, Alec," he continued with a chuckle. "Know what I was just thinking, son? The world is so huge, Alec. It's so huge that there's probably a thousand guys like me sitting there mourning their dead wife right at this very second, and a thousand wives mourning their dead husbands. They're all sat looking up at the stars just like me, and you know what? I find some comfort in that."

He got up to walk inside before I could ask anything else, and I just stayed out there for a while. He was right. Putting the world into perspective was important when feeling down. Looking back there were plenty of times I could've eased my anger or made better decisions had I thought about the bigger picture, but I was young then.

Either way, in that moment my body was cold, but my mind... my mind was fixated on that room. The feeling that the room gave off—it didn't really feel like the end. Maybe a release, maybe a solace.

My grandparents were the heads of our family: They were what made us, what contained us. All that stuff around the house, all those things. That house is a memory. A big messy memory of all things good and all things bad, and they just walked around knowing and feeling it all, all the time. I wouldn't judge them; I couldn't. No one could.

My grandfather was right. We're all hoarders, whether we like to admit it or not. We may not show it, not to the extent that people can't see our floors, or that we have mounds of regret piling up, but we're hoarders. He was also right that it is inevitable. My grandparents aren't hoarders by fault, but by the stark reality that life barrels up inside of us until we can't hide anymore.

I started back toward my truck. The large black frame almost shined bright enough to look good in its moon-lit rendition. I was quickly reassured of its state, however, when I turned the single key that was permanently stuck in the ignition and waited nearly ten seconds for the engine to turn over. Being in my senior year of high school, I didn't expect to be driving something brand new, but this was just sad.

My mom approached my window just as I was about to shift into reverse. "Hey, honey. How are you?" she started, her voice cracked and frail.

We weren't the closest family. In her middle age she just seemed to fit into her routine as most middle-aged people do. I wondered, though, what she was hiding or, rather, carrying. Had she lived a totally different life before me? Had her memories been stained, or were they happier than the reality she lived in now?

"Fine. Just feel bad for Grandpa is all. I told Aaron I'd go by his house for a beer and then I'll head home, all right?" I muttered in response.

She hadn't any opposition to my plan, contrary to her usual lecture about drinking and driving. It always ended with a harsh exchange between us and my final defeat after slamming the door behind me and starting toward wherever I intended to go. I don't blame her as I wasn't of age anyway when I started drinking, but it's just because of who I was exposed to in high school. My parents never were harsh on me; that's the thing. As soon as I said I was going to a friend's house and may have a beer, however, it was a totally different story.

"Just be home early enough so you can wake up for the service tomorrow. Trust me, I hate these things just as much as you do. I can't remember the last funeral I've been to since your uncle," she said, looking down and turning away instantly. The transition was odd, but given the circumstance I guess everyone acted oddly that day, so I, too, went on my way.

I put the truck in reverse and started toward Aaron's house. I couldn't stop thinking about my grandfather—what he said out on that bench. Like he meant for me to repent or meant for me to think about everything I ever did wrong. What do we hoard? Everything, I guess. What we could have said instead of being afraid, how we could've won that game, ended that fight. It could've always gone better, I guess.

When I arrived at Aaron's, I wasn't surprised to see more than one car parked in his driveway. Aaron always did that, and it was my fault for ever thinking anything would be different. He would invite me over with the inclination that we're going to have a couple drinks and watch a movie. I accept and he immediately takes to the phone and invites all our other friends. I don't mind any of them, but I don't mind being without them either.

I walked into the house to be welcomed with the sorrowful greetings of people who had been dancing and screaming minutes before. I reassured them all that we could forget about death for the night and live for something else—live for the moment we were in instead of dying to understand what the hell was going on every second of our lives. And to that, we downed a shot of whatever Aaron poured us.

"I am so sorry, Alec. After all your family has been through, I can only imagine how this feels," Misty said. She was almost my mom's age, hanging around Aaron like some older mentor with benefits. Not the ideal scenario, but I tried not to judge.

My family? What was she talking about? I started toward the case of beers and took a seat in the living room, content on being alone. Lo and behold, there she was, springing toward me like a lioness on its prey. Carrie, that is.

"Are you okay?" she asked, halfheartedly.

She was a nice girl. Dark brown hair ran down her shoulders. She was very pretty, but her personality wasn't exactly one you'd dream about. Looks that turned heads but conversations so dull that you wished you had left it at a simple hello. I shouldn't say that; she wasn't a mean person by any means. With her left knee rubbing on mine and her one hand brushing the top of my hair, I assumed from my lack of movement she'd get the message, but she continued.

"I mean, about your grandma. I remember when my grandma died. I didn't even go to the funeral. I hate…"

The more she went on and on the more I drank. One beer led to two and pretty soon an entire six pack was coursing through my bloodstream. That was definitely my cue to leave. As if I had anything else to report on my exciting night, I didn't even get to talk to Aaron. He was too busy with Misty, and I didn't try to intervene. I considered staying the night because of how much I drank, then remembered that my mom would kill me if she didn't find me in the morning.

By this time, Carrie had gone over to grab another drink. Perfect timing for the perfect Irish goodbye. "I'll see you guys later," I muttered to myself in my half-in-the-bag random accent of the evening.

Either I'd had one too many beers or my truck was back in its original glory, because it started faster than one of Carrie's stories. I could barely see on my way home due to a thick cloud of fog corrupting the view of the road. I'd done this many times before, drinking and driving. It isn't a good thing to say you're good at, but better than saying you're bad.

I was about a mile from my house when suddenly a deer came up onto the right side of the road. I pulled the wheel hard to the left and felt the tires lose their traction with the road. My heart sank into the pit of my stomach, and for one second, I felt all the regret of my decision until finally I regained control. The left tires made contact with the sidewalk, but it wasn't enough to derail me. The regret was quickly replaced with the feeling of sheer adrenaline. Like I was some sort of Formula One race car driver, I continued with pace.

I turned the radio on and blasted whatever was playing at three o'clock in the morning. Windows down and a whole lot of luck behind me, I pushed my arm out the window and felt the breeze against my skin. It was brisk and cold, but the alcohol masked that pain. I turned corners with flawless ease and darted down straightaways faster than I ever believed possible for the same truck that barely started just a day before.

I was instantly pulled back to earth by a memory I'd buried from years earlier, and when it hit me, it slowed me to a pace so inconsistent with how I had previously been driving that I could feel my own disappointment brooding. However cool I thought I was, I also knew what I was doing was wrong. I passed all the most familiar houses in the world, in my world. What my grandfather said could apply to anything. Somewhere out there a kid was driving home just as I was, looking at houses he had passed for his entire life on the way home from school, from late night soccer practices, from his first date.

Pulling into my driveway directly after muting the stereo, I got down from the truck and tiptoed across the lawn. My parents' room was directly over the driveway, so I didn't even think to get close to the house. That was too close an encounter to be comfortable with, but not bad enough that I'd learn. Before I knew it, I was fast asleep.

Chapter 2

———

I awoke to my regular alarm, my head pounding as if an inflatable balloon was growing inside. Eight o'clock sharp and I turned over to meet the clink of a few bottles crashing into each other at the foot of my bed. I guess I lied to myself. I hadn't gone right to bed, I just followed up what I started over at Aaron's. I sat up, rubbing my forehead with the might of placebo doing absolutely nothing to redeem the pain.

If I'm being honest, drinking wasn't a normal thing to my family. My parents would have one or two when we were at parties or events, but nothing at home. Once I turned eighteen and Aaron started hanging around older people more often, we just did it to pass the time. Living in a small town, other than frequenting the usual restaurants, all we did over the summer was go to the rope swing a few minutes from my house. All we did at the rope swing was swim and drink, and since we could walk there, we didn't have to worry about how to get home.

I was never shy by any means, but Aaron and I didn't have many other friends at our high school. I still remember our first day of ninth grade, they separated us after home room and we both ran to the bathroom and played with our trading cards rather than being in a class without each other. Obviously as we grew older we learned to do things on our own, but the influence Aaron had on my life was still fairly substantial. He grew up in foster care and got adopted when he was twelve. I met him his first day in town and we instantly bonded over our fascination with the same super villain, the Galactic Invader. I never took down his poster; it was always hung up in my closet, next to the gaming set we used to use every night until my mom forced us off. Aaron was like the brother I never had growing up, and I didn't need much more than him to keep myself occupied.

Eighteen was a weird time for me. I was just learning to put myself out there with women. I wanted to be a tough and confident young man, but I always found myself second guessing bad decisions that others would make to seem "cool" and be accepted. Overthinking every single thing I did usually led me to staying in my comfort zone, hanging out with Aaron, and not getting any jobs other than working in my dad's shop over the summer.

I was lucky to have a room at the top of my house. Every morning I rolled out of bed and my routine commenced. I had a coffee maker right by the window, which lead out to a balcony overlooking our backyard. The pot would brew, and I would race to beat it as I washed my face and brushed my teeth. By the time I turned the sink off to pat dry my face I always heard the last sputter or two of the coffee maker, and then the drips went silent, showing I had once again been defeated by modern technology. It was pretty sad, honestly.

Eighteen years old in a small town racing against a brewing pot for fun in the morning and hanging out with my only friend by night.

That was one of the highlights of my day, though. Seeing the steam roll toward open air as the coffee was brewing, directing me toward where I would be headed. I was always content in my room, confiding in my loneliness and feeling safe by the invisible barrier that was created around the four walls. When I was in there, I had more privacy than any other place in the world. Being an only child had some obvious perks—picking that upstairs room that my parents previously barred me from accessing was one of them. They always told me I couldn't stay up there until I finally begged enough that they gave up on my eighteenth birthday.

I had never been up there before besides one time when my mother and I were playing hide and seek as a kid. I ran up the stairs, hid behind a large box, and heard an instant panic in my mother's voice when she realized I was nowhere else in the house but there. It puzzled me, but they closed the room off to me—blaming the caution of the outside patio being a hazard at my age—and then finally reopened the room for me to move into that year. The patio became an instant place of comfort for me to go to, higher than any point besides the roof and giving a view that I could always enjoy privately. Something about being the only person who saw those trees and that animal from that distinct point of view in the world gave me a sense of advantage over everyone else. Contrary to what my grandfather told me at the funeral, there may be another person in the world going through something close to you, but never the same. No one had the vantage point that

I had; no one could see and imagine and feel the things that I did on a daily basis.

I got back to the coffee pot, added my flavor of choice, and took my mug outside. The air was cold. There wasn't any snow yet, but we'd be expecting some soon. Seeing my breath wasn't enough to distract me from the beauty of the outdoors. The leaves weren't molten red yet, but the grass was a faded green. Dew turned to frost as the day brought more frigid air than before. In moments like those, I put the world into perspective.

In moments like those, I was always forced to think deeply about what I was doing in the world. I was still in school. I didn't know about college. Not for me, I guess. My dad owned a garage he inherited after my uncle passed away. I could always just work there after I finish school. Monday through Friday I went to that garage and learned all the ins and outs of many different cars. Aaron and I had been helping my dad out there since we were fourteen. It brought all of us closer together.

Together when my father wasn't the "together" kind of person. He always worked, was always there, but not much past that. During times like those nights in the garage, he and I were able to actually share a laugh, talk about girls, toss a football across the open hood of whatever car we were working on.

It definitely saved me some money too. That damned truck would've cost me my life savings had I not known so much about fixing the stupid thing.

My dad was entranced by that place. My uncle and him had been obsessed with cars since they were young. My mom says they were closer than anyone she ever knew—inseparable.

My dad told me when my uncle died in a street racing accident, he vowed to continue their legacy but in the right way. He even took care of my cousins and aunt. All the money that he made from the shop he split with them.

I respect my dad for that—being able to work for your family and other people, getting up every day knowing you'll make just enough to get by for yourself and others. It took some commitment and bravery. Reasons like that were why I justified his distance from me. I was his only child, but he was never the fun type of dad. Throwing the football outside or going out to breakfast didn't seem like the things he enjoyed doing. "Work was a substitute for all sin," he said. "Work was the only place where you never do anything wrong as long as you get your job done."

In times like these, I also liked to pray. I was never super religious, but the feeling of knowing there is something out there looking down on you was comforting. Knowing that you could say a few words and feel like there was some sort of force field around you had helped me when I was younger, and I guess I just never let go of that feeling. I used to pray because when I watched a scary movie, I didn't want any monsters to get me. If I said the right words to the right being, I felt like I was safe from everything I'd otherwise fear.

The air was brittle, but it still stung the parts of me that were exposed openly. I couldn't smell much. You never really can when it's cold. I never understand it, but I got used to that from sitting out here. In the summer I can smell the trees, and something is always being carried in the air. Either the smell of a barbecue, plants emitting their natural odor, something more than just the cold.

I turned back and headed into my room to get dressed. The suit and tie that my mother had rented me were perfectly pressed waiting for me on my desk chair. I slipped them on and looked in the mirror at myself. Maybe being a businessman and wearing a suit every day wouldn't be so bad. Or maybe an assassin. Assassins wear suits too.

It was my father's mother who died. You would've thought she was my mother's mom, though; they were closer than anyone in the family. I guess it was nice compared to the way that everyone always refers to mother in-laws hating their sons' wives for making them the second most important women in their lives. Whenever she and my mom were together it was as if they picked up from the second their last conversation left off. My father, on the other hand, had a different relationship with his parents.

I always caught him looking down when he was in front of them. Whenever they came to family parties, he just hugged them and then nodded his head, walking back away from them. I assumed it was just the way they were, just like how my father wasn't super affectionate with me.

When we all got out the front door, I saw my mother whip her head back and pierce me with her gaze. My truck was halfway onto the grass, without a doubt exposing my state of mind when I got home the night before. Due to the day, I think she just decided to let it go, and they got into the car following behind me as we went back to the funeral home.

My grandfather could still drive, so he met us there. I saw his twenty-five-year-old station wagon parked in the first spot at the funeral home as we were pulling in. There he was, sorrowful eyes gazing forward at the building where his wife lay. He pressed a flask to his lips again. My god it was only nine in the morning, but again, due to the day, I just decided to let it go and didn't give it another thought. I did wonder, though, if his drinking influenced the lack thereof in my father. If he starts this early in the morning, maybe it was a problem when my father was younger. Maybe that's also something my grandfather carries around, something he hoards inside.

The services passed as all others do. Somber faces paired with the sounds of one or two sobbing attendees always breaking the silence that ensued. We all prayed in unison, shared a few laughs, and ultimately it was time to move out to the cemetery.

My grandparents were a part of a local church that had a plot of land that was also local. They were the first generation of my family to live here in this small town. As we were driving through, everyone stopped and stared at the hearse as it rolled down the dainty and quiet streets. The autumn leaves were perfectly colored, foliage so beautiful it distracted from the gray sky above us. Past Mr. Jenkins's meat market, he stood with his hat between his hands, his head lowered looking to the floor. If there was one good thing about Wellspring, it was that everyone was respectful of one another. We hadn't had any large-scale crimes or heinous acts since I could remember, and everyone got along, sometimes too well. Trying to keep a secret in my town was like hanging clothes out to dry in the rain, or so I thought.

When we brought my grandmother to the cemetery there was a different tone in the environment. I climbed down from the truck and turned to the eerie and silent tones it emitted. As soon as my bumper passed the main gate it was like something in the air shifted. Branches hung from trees swaying in the wind brooding over the deceased below them. They must've been older than the oldest people buried there, shedding their leaves for hundreds of years before we arrived. The trees were rooted there, stuck for all of eternity, and so too now would my grandmother.

Humans are the only animals on the earth that have graveyards. We're the only animals that normalized celebrating the passing of life and memorializing it. What made our relationships more important and necessary to celebrate on days like this than any others? What do monkeys or alligators do with their dead? The moss and decay on some of the older tombstones was a relic to the true complexity of death and how old this practice really was.

As I continued behind the hearse, watching the pallbearers take the casket from the rear, my eyes fixed on my grandfather. He was much more distraught than he had been when we were at the house. This was the end, the realization that she was going to her final resting place, and I knew he felt that pain; he internalized everything they ever had and ever spoke about. My aunt hugged my mom. "It's been so long since we've been here. Almost twenty years now. Are you going to tell him today?" she whispered, looking toward me.

My father took me by the hand, a weird gesture compared to his usual lack of display. When the priest said his prayer of committal the casket was being lowered into the ground, and my aunt approached me.

"Now you see what they always hide. There's always something to hide in your damn family!" she whispered in a tone so loud it startled me and others around me. My mother must've noticed her and quickly creeped over to us, grabbing her by the hand and obviously demanding her to stop.

She looked to my father. "I told them to cover the damn headstone! How hard was it to just cover the headstone?" she muttered quietly in panic.

"Alec, there is something I need to tell you." Before she could continue, I saw it. As they lowered my grandmother's casket down far enough to see the gravestone, I read the inscription.

With Love Always, Never Forget You: David Godfrey 1985–2003, John Godfrey 1960–2003

David Godfrey? My uncle was John, but a David? Died in 2003. I was born in 2003. I felt a panging in my chest. I looked around. Everyone was peering at me. My aunt was screaming, "You should've told him! I told you to tell him! What's the matter with you people?"

Everyone was in shock by the scene she was creating. It was a funeral, and she was screaming and taking everybody's attention. The air felt colder than ice, the wind piercing my extremities. I was so confused and lost in her episode. But the name on the tombstone—who is that? Who is now beside my grandmother's place of rest?

I turned away in disbelief, my eyes darting at the ground below me. What was I supposed to do? Run? Stay and not make a scene? It was my grandmother's funeral; I couldn't add any more tragedy to the day. I looked to my aunt. "Please, let's just leave this for now. We have a family member to bury. One I actually know about! Let's not make this day any worse, please," I said.

I wanted to know. I was more than curious, more than enraged. All my life I had another family member that my parents never told me about. I was sure the explanation was simpler than I made it out to be. Maybe he was my aunt's son, and she kept it from me. But no, she said it was my parents that held the blame.

My aunt stormed off and slammed the car door behind her, driving off without my cousins. Katie and Elizabeth were their names. They stood frozen, staring at me. They were twins, more than double my age. They didn't drive themselves, so my mother turned to them and told them to follow her to the car. I looked to her and turned to them without an exchange; not to be rude, I was more just in shock at how this all ended. I felt bad for my father as he watched his mother being laid to rest, but I feel like he was at peace with it.

My grandfather was the most upset. Bent to his knees, he was weeping over her grave, crying tears down into that hole.

Right now, that hole they were dropping her in was all he could think about.

My mind was scattering. My grandfather, my aunt, everyone else in attendance—I had no clue where to turn. I was so upset that I was so confused, and I went to my grandfather to ask if he was okay. He turned to me and said, his voice trembling, "I told you, son. We all have things we hoard. Whether up here," pointing to his head, "or out there in front of us," pointing down toward the grave.

I tried my hardest not to make a scene of anything. I pulled out my phone and flipped open the top, revealing a message from a few friends from school wishing me luck, saying they were thinking about me. I tried to make as little eye contact as possible with anyone and respected my grandfather's time to be at peace before whatever needed to break loose did.

"Just meet us at your aunts afterward. Okay, Alec?" my mother asked.

I nodded. Not to be rude, just that the anger and discomfort had swept through me. I had a pounding in my chest so thorough that I wanted to lash out. I was angry at my aunt, and I was angry at my family. How many people knew about this other than me? Is this why everyone was staring at me when I walked into the cemetery? So much for a town that can't hold a secret.

I looked up, and the trees were twisting in the wind, the sun fully pocketed by the clouds in front of it. I turned to my cousins and waved them over to me as I started back to my truck.

When we arrived at their house, my aunt was in the driveway arguing with my mother. My mother had her hand over her face, my aunt yelling down at her. My father was in the car behind them, just looking forward in silence. I felt bad for him. This isn't the day he hoped for, but why didn't he tell me, either? There had to be a perfectly sound explanation for all of it.

"Can we forget about this for now? I don't think I am the only one who thinks Grandpa deserves a simple day. When he pulls in, I don't want him to see everyone fighting. Do you guys?" I asked, trying to suppress the situation.

For the remainder of the day, I went along trying to act as normal as possible. No one brought up the name I read on the tombstone, and I didn't either. Anger wasn't what I felt anymore; the ride helped to disperse some of the hurt. I was still nosy, however, and I scoured the house for any photo or album I could that may have a hint of who that guy was to my aunt and her family.

I finally gave up and sat in the middle of the family room. I peered around at faces I barely knew and realized how odd families are. We come together for life and death, and in between we just all go about our lives, racing around like we don't have enough time to spend one day together. It made days like that feel like they had less integrity. Our tiny town with its little history didn't help, either, and that's why I didn't have much as far as memories from my childhood.

My middle school math teacher arrived, as well as the librarian. That sparked one memory, if anything.

My mother used to take me to the library every Sunday evening. We would all sit around and read from a children's book. The library was so long, and the shelves seemed to rise higher than I thought possible for anyone to reach. I used to imagine I'd never be tall enough to read the books that hid at the highest point on each shelf. She tried to get me to read, to write, to do anything that would inspire an artistic side. She had a painting room at the base of our house. While my father worked at the shop, my mother would make professional portraits for people in our town.

One time the mayor of Wellspring invited us over for dinner, and my mother painted a portrait of all his children with him that night. I stood back eating cookies that the in-home chef baked for us. I still remember the taste, a savory aroma of chocolate and pillowy dough that melted in the back of my throat.

Other than art I can't remember many passions that my mother had. She even looked like a worn-out artist. Her frazzled black hair complemented by an all-too-familiar paint splotched pair of overalls, with one clip unhooked and a white shirt underneath. It was like she had an endless supply of this outfit on hand.

We all lived in the same house but were separated mentally. They were so careful with me when it came to going out or leaving the house, but then when I was there, we didn't do much together, either. I wasn't even allowed to sleep over at a friend's now that I look back. Aaron was allowed to sleep over whenever he wanted, and that was about it.

The librarian approached me from out of nowhere. "Hi, Alec. How are you, sweetie?" she asked. Ms. Genine was a tall, slender woman. Her golden hair beamed under her light, soft blue eyes that made her perfect as the comforting librarian who read stories to children in her spare time.

"I'm all right. Thank you. I just have a lot on my mind." And before I could get out another thought, she started. The book clubs at the library would apparently be my best bet as far as getting my mind off mourning. Reading was a passage to another dimension, a way to get yourself lost in the words. I understood that. But something about not seeing it in front of me didn't allow it to hold my attention for long enough. I couldn't take much more talk about books, and I had to get back to my main objective. "Excuse me, Ms. Genine, I think the bucket the drinks are in needs some refreshing! I'll be right back!" I said. "I'm going to go get more ice from downstairs!" I yelled to them in the other room.

When I got to the bottom of the stairs, I peered just past the refrigerator to a pile of boxes. Maybe they were filled with old photos. Why I hadn't thought to check down there earlier was beyond me. I went through all the trouble of tiptoeing through the top floor of the house totally disregarding the one place where secrets are stored.

I took one last look up the stairs. Everyone was conversating and caught up in the day, so I was clear to take a look. The first few boxes were all old clothes. The first cover revealed a shriveled boutonniere on a suit from years ago, probably my uncle's from their wedding day. I opted not to touch such a sentimental piece and moved on to the next box. I found old diaries and mechanic records from when he and my father owned their shop. My uncle kept a diary? It seemed odd that a grown man would find comfort in writing down his thoughts. I flipped to the first page.

I am not a great man. I am far from a perfect father. I am less of a great brother. My brother is my keeper. He and I, when we're in that shop doing our thing, the whole world collapses around us. This is nothing but a bleak coincidence. Just a minor wrinkle in the world, and it can be ironed out. Any problem can. I'm sure he doesn't even know. I don't know how I would even tell him, anyway. Why would I have to, after all. As long as that kid doesn't find out, we'll be good to keep on going until the end of the year.

I flipped the page, and there was a photo. A child that couldn't have been more than five or six, held by my father. That wasn't me, though; that was much earlier than when I was born. My father was holding him, my aunt holding the twins.

The next box was filled with—

"Alec, you having trouble down there? If the ice machine doesn't work, there should be some bags in a boat cooler just past the fridge. Do you need help?" I heard my aunt yell from the top step.

I slowly and silently placed the cover back on the box and shifted around just in time for her last step to reach the basement floor.

"I guess I'm just thinking too much. I got caught in the silence down here. Today was a really heavy day is all," I explained to her.

"I know, Alec. And I really am sorry for how I acted earlier. You have to understand, this family… there is a lot you don't know about. It isn't something you can just hide from someone who is already an adult like yourself. I was just angry because of the circumstance. Please don't be offended, all right?" she said to me. I could hear the sincerity in her tone. I felt bad for her, understanding the baseline of what I was ignorant of. "Let's go back upstairs. Here, grab these bags of ice. I'll take the other two," she started.

I still didn't know. Still didn't know how to feel. My uncle's diary. Who was he talking about? Where was this going? I had to ask my parents before the day was over. This can't be hidden any longer. When my aunt and I got to the top step, my mother motioned for me to go to the back deck with her, and I followed, my father close behind me.

Chapter 3

———

We stepped out onto my aunt's back porch. I took a seat next to my father, who just sat with his head down. My mother stood facing us, a determined look on her face. I could tell she was going to do all the talking—she usually did anyway. I was beyond mad with my father. Even now he didn't want to connect with me, didn't want to sit his son down and have this talk. Instead, he sat with his eyes glued to the floor. I saw him as a coward in that moment. That was before I knew.

The patio chair was cold under my legs, panging through my jeans, I was waiting for my body heat to warm it below me. I breathed a cloud into the open air, trying to allude to the cold and shake the awkward silence that ensued.

"Honey, we can either tell you this in full from the beginning, or you can ask us whatever you want," she started.

I thought about asking her outright who David was and why they kept this from me for so long. I wanted her to get to the point, though I wanted to hear the whole truth. "Let me just hear it from the beginning, please," I asked.

"David was your brother. He... is your brother. He... he just isn't with us anymore," she started.

Well, there was a fifty percent chance that he was my brother or my aunt's son. I didn't make a face, although I was hiding a wave of emotions behind my locked tongue. I stayed silent until she continued.

"I mean, honey, did you ever think about the fact that your father and I were pretty much older than the rest of the parents around?" she asked.

I won't lie, I never really did think about it, although having parents that age was as normal as having ones that were younger because it was all that I knew. My mother was thirty-eight when she had me, my father already forty. Even though it seemed like an age that you wouldn't strive for to start a family, it wasn't something out of the ordinary to me.

"David had some trouble growing up. This is a small town, honey. You know that. Your father and I were still kids, our early twenties, when he was growing up. Not many choices for schools, friends. You kind of get what you get. Anyway, David didn't have the best friends in high school, and he acted out a lot. When he was sixteen, he started drinking and didn't stop unless I caught him. He would drink and party like it was the only thing he cared about, and we couldn't change his mind on any of it. When he got old enough to get a job, we decided we would send him to where your uncle and aunt used to live about an hour and a half west of here. We got him a job working in your uncle's old shop. We decided it would be a good thing if he had some discipline, and maybe—you never know—he could fall in love with the garage."

She went on to explain to me a story that seemed like it was stolen out of a movie I watched, or a dream—no, a nightmare. My uncle owed money to people in this town, wherever it was. She said he took a loan out to keep himself afloat, but it still wasn't enough. The diary, the diary down in the basement. That's what he was talking about. Just a wrinkle that needed to be ironed out.

She said that my brother always had money saved, and that one day my uncle stole the money from him to pay back the loan. For some reason, and this one I still can't fully comprehend, David was working with the men who loaned my uncle the money. They told David to check his savings and ultimately found out what my uncle had done. My uncle didn't die in a street racing accident. There was an accident, but nothing of his doing.

My mother continued, "David was so infuriated that he stormed back to the house with the group of men to scare your uncle into paying him on the spot. If he never stole that stupid money…! If he just came to us, or… or… I don't know… anyway. David acted out of rage, or fear, or I don't know. It was a… it was a mistake, Alec. You have to know that." She stopped, tripping on her words as she started to weep.

"What happened, mom? What did he *do*?" I demanded.

My father, eyes still glued to the ground, turned to me and started, "David and those men he came with met your uncle in his office above the garage; they dangled him over the ledge outside his window. They were trying to intimidate him. David had turned against the one man who was trying to change his life, who was trying to make him better. Even better than I would have made him... When David went to shake him, they both lost their grip, and your uncle fell. He... didn't make it."

I kept my silence, and after a brief pause he said, "We didn't tell you this because we didn't know how to. How do I tell my own son that his older brother killed their uncle? How did anyone expect me to tell you this?"

I felt a tingling in my skin like I was starting to sweat. Despite the cold, warmth was building in my body, welling in my eyes. I was fighting back the tears, trying to keep a steady pace with my breathing. In shock, I stayed still picking at the corner of my fingernails. I didn't want them to see it. I spread my fingers and started rubbing them back and forth across my thighs until I let out a simple question, "And David? What happened to David?"

My mother's cry came to a halt. "We don't need to—"

"What happened to David?" I screamed, instantly hanging my head in embarrassment of my outrage.

"Your brother ran off in shock of what happened, and he died in a car accident. The other men said they would take care of your uncle's... his body, that David just needed to get out of town for a few weeks. They would pin it on themselves and no one would know. Your brother drove off and died on his way back from our cabin another hour or so west of the garage. He had been drinking, but the shock is what got to him. He sat in that cabin alone for weeks, drinking and regretting his choices, I'm sure. There weren't any cars on the road with him. That cabin is on one of the least busy roads in the state. We never really knew if it was the alcohol or the regret, or if he chose his fate right in that moment," she said.

"So, if you never shipped him off to their house, if you knew how to raise a child, none of this would've happened!" I screamed.

My father started, "Well, Alec, I never was a perfect person. After you were born, though, I really changed my life around, and I—"

"Just forget it!" I let out. "I don't even know who I am, who he is. Why did everyone go this long without telling me anything?"

I got up, and the dizziness subsided and left itself stinging in my knees. I turned to my parents, both crying and looking down to their feet. I did feel for them. I really didn't like to see them in pain. Obviously this isn't what they wanted, but I didn't know what to do for them. Why didn't they do anything to make it easier for me? I turned to the backyard and started around the house back to my truck.

I got up into the seat and turned the key, driving off as fast as I could. The sun was sinking, and the clouds were starting to transition to their nightly routine as I sped away from the house. My fingers struggled to clasp the steering wheel, the shock wildly forcing twitches on the ends of my hands and sudden bursts in my hips and thighs. I pulled to the side of the road about a mile or two from my house and stared into the woods before me. I couldn't go home, couldn't go see my parents the same way, not right now. It wasn't the time or the day to do this.

I called Aaron. "Hey, man. Can't explain much but meet me at Sully's in ten. Just trust me. I need to see you." And without hesitation, he affirmed and hung up.

Sully's had been our favorite place since Aaron and I learned to drive. He and I had a job there for one day. So much for trying to get out of our comfort zone. We soon realized it was much more fun being patrons then getting screamed at for hours on end by the owner. Sully Jr. was a short, fat man, balding as fast as the gray subsided on what hair was left on his head and mustache. He was a company man, always walking around with his stained apron, talking up the regulars. He would make our specialty without Aaron and I asking, and that's what awaited us as soon as we arrived.

I got down in front of Aaron at our usual booth. "Hey, man. I just told SJ to bring us the regular before you got here. You hungry?" he asked, but I knew he was curious.

Before I had a single bite of our famous Sully's skillet I told him everything. If it had been any other time, the twin burgers, mound of waffle fries, and chicken tender concoction we had created when we used to work here would be wiped clean. It was all served on a large cast iron because Sully always used to run out of plates when we worked there, so we resorted to using what we had. Like I said, tasted a lot better as patrons then it did when we were getting screamed out to whiff it down and get back to work.

Anyway, I just blurted out to Aaron every last detail of what my parents said and how the funeral went and so on. I looked around the diner as he absorbed all that I told him. The entire atmosphere felt different. Neon red and blue lights that darted around every corner of the room seemed to shine a lot less bright than they had when we were younger. Aaron and I used to go to that diner and spend endless hours making up our own Galactic Invader sketches, talking about what we wanted to do with our lives—what it would be like to move far away from here.

"I don't know what to say, man. I—I feel like I can't really say this... but—"

I cut in, "What? Dude, listen, I've had enough people telling me that today. If there's something you can say, just say it."

"You know that girl I've been seeing? Well, she kind of told me about the whole thing. Last night at the party, after you left, she went on and on about some shit your parents were hiding from you. Apparently, she used to babysit your brother back when he was, like, eight or nine. She said your parents kind of forced her to keep it a secret. Some sort of court thing," he went on.

"Anyway, man. By the end of the night, she said your parents were planning to cover up a gravestone next to your grandma's today. I thought about you, man. I just thought about the brother I never had. I never knew shit about my parents, and it pissed me off that they would try to do the same to you with your brother. This morning right before everyone got to the cemetery, I ripped off that stupid cover they put over the headstone. I know it was wrong. I know it didn't do anything good for the service, but it gave you the truth, man. It showed you what they were trying to hide from you, bro."

I looked around, confused; not angry, just puzzled as to how many people were in on this other than myself. I shot up out of the seat and put my arms out. Aaron stood up and hugged me, "Thanks, man. Only a true brother would do that for me."

Without asking another question I sat back down and split our favorite meal.

"How about your grandfather, man? I mean, grandparents know everything. The same way your mom and dad know everything for the last fifty years or so, your grandparents know double that. I couldn't imagine being that old. Knowing everything your kids do, living with it, and then everything your kids' kids do. Man, I couldn't keep up with it," he went on.

He was right, though—my grandfather. He'd left the house well before I did. Couldn't stand to be around my family and see us there sitting and mourning; it wouldn't have helped him, anyway. He'd been there from the beginning, though. He must have all the answers.

"I'm gonna go see him, man. Thank you. Truly," I said, and with that I got up and started back toward my truck.

I pulled in the front driveway and saw smoke from the backyard. I walked toward it. A fire was going in the pit, and he was sitting by it with a large coat on, clenching his fingers around his flask. I started toward him, grabbing a folding chair on my way and posting it right beside him. He handed me the flask without a second thought. As sick to my stomach as I felt, the warmth of the whiskey working its way down my throat provided the littlest consolation in that moment.

"They told me," I muttered. "They told me, and I don't know what to do."

"And what can you do, exactly?" he asked. "What exactly do you think you can do now? Your father and mother, they spent eighteen years trying to raise someone who never accepted their love. Your grandmother and I, we lost sixty total years of raising a child and looking after a grand-child. But you? You heard a story that could've been right out of anyone's imagination because you were never there and never saw any of it, any of it!" he said in a brisk and unforgiving tone.

I hadn't gone there to get lectured. He wasn't wrong, though. "I just feel betrayed. I feel like they should've told me. I know it won't bring anyone back, but it just all makes sense now. My father inheriting all the money for a new shop, doing what he and my uncle loved. Sending money to my aunt and cousins. Why did he do that?" I asked.

"Your father hasn't looked a single person in this family right in their eyes since what happened. Your father wakes up and goes to sleep with the idea of his own son killing his brother, his best friend. He tried with you, and he's doing a hell of a job. Whether or not you think he's always around to kick a ball with you or take you to the movies, you're a hell of a kid compared to your older brother," he said.

"I just want answers. I just want to see him—to see them, I guess. I don't know what I want right now," I said. "The cabin he went to—what were they talking about? They said he went to a cabin a few hours from here."

"It's not a cabin. It's nothing special, but it's a house. It was my house," he said.

A cigar made its way over the arm of his chair, and he pressed it to his lips, curling his cheeks in and out and letting out a slow rolling cloud. He looked up into the stars; the clouds had dispersed, showing every star in the sky.

"Do you know what my father used to tell me when I was a kid? That cabin was set up on a mountain. Not right up there, but higher elevation than here. And he used to tell me that for every star in the sky, there was one ancestor who was looking right back down to us. For every star in the sky, I had a grandfather, an aunt or uncle, all looking right back at my every move. I saw God in these stars, Alec. Every time I press a flask to my lips in open air, smoke a cigar, they can see me doing it. I came out here tonight so your grandmother could watch me, look down on me and see what I was doing, see that I'm all right without her being here, even if I'm drowning myself in booze," he said, letting out a swift chuckle.

"Well, have you been there since—since David died?" I asked.

"No one has. Not one of us has been there. I know how to get in, though. I know for a fact it's inhabitable. We never got rid of that house because I never lost the rights. It's so far off the main road anyway that no one wants it or knows about it. Must've been why David thought it was such a good idea to go there. We kept it hidden from the police too. When they did their investigation, we acted like we didn't have any clue where he went off to. But we did."

"Grandpa, please. I need to go there. I need to see it." I asked, taking another swig off his flask. "I can't be around here right now, and who knows, maybe I'll find something to do with him, anything."

"Oh, you'll find something at least. Like I said, the place is inhabitable, but it's untouched. You might actually find what he left behind if no one's been there yet," he said.

"Please tell me. Grandpa, please. I don't want to go back home tonight. I don't even know what I'd say to my parents right now."

He took the flask from my hands, following another puff of his cigar with a swig of whiskey. His face shone as a reflection of the flames. I could see him contemplating the decision.

"If you come up to the house—and this is if you find it, by the way—you might, and I mean might, see a small plastic turtle like a garden statue off the front porch. Lift it up and there's a panel that comes off the bottom. Key's in there. Like I said, if it's not yet a dump for squatters or a family of wolves, do what you want, but for the love of Christ don't tell your parents I let you go there!"

"If they ask, tell them I went to Syd's house. Please just do it!" I exclaimed.

"That the girl you used to bring around for a few months? Didn't you guys break up last summer or so?" he asked.

"Yes, please, just leave it and tell them. They'll think I went to visit her at school for a few days or something."

I could tell he already felt liable for all that. I looked down and then thanked him and started back toward the front of the house. When I got into the truck, I could see him from the front windshield, sitting and looking up at the stars. I presumed he was trying to figure out—to figure out which one she was and whether she was looking down on him yet. If what he said was true, I hoped David was looking down on me, thinking what in the world I might be doing going to dig into his life.

I backed out of the driveway and headed down the street. My grandfather told me it was about eighty miles east, down the main highway until I found a sign for Lacoy National Park, and when I got there, I took the next exit and just followed the first access road as far as it landed until I found the house.

One star shone brightest in the sky, straight up ahead of me. They say if you stare long enough at the North Star all the other stars revolve around it. I wondered if everyone saw different north stars. If someone in the world was someone's North Star, and all their ancestors and all their family revolved around them.

Chapter 4

———

The night sky dwindled, and the stars began to hide behind neatly connected clouds. Overcast subsided, and it didn't take a weather report to see what would soon follow. The first drop slapped my windshield so hard that for a second I thought it could've been hail. The subsequent drops got stronger and more forceful as they came. My personal flask—the one I hid in the glove box—was almost empty, and my eyes were flickering more times than the rain itself was falling. I had to find somewhere to stop.

After some time, suddenly a light shone through the trees on the left side of the road. I pulled up to a clearing and met a gas station with its lights still blinking—left to right, left to right—set to catch the eye. Like the gates of heaven at the perfect time, catch the eye it did. Whether I was in the middle of a rainstorm or in broad sunlight I wouldn't miss this place. The sign must've been twice the length of the truck. "SHOP OPEN," it read along the horizon of the roof. At its base I was met with more gas pumps than I figured there were cars in this entire town and a stack of tires maybe twelve high, higher than any person would be able to get down or stack up for that matter.

I parked under the overhang and peered to my left into the garage. Coming out of the truck, the alcohol didn't help my step, but my adrenaline and it being the middle of the morning paired with approaching a mysterious wonder-garage was enough to keep one foot in front of the other. Too good to be true was an understatement, and I darted to the door through the rain faster than I'd be able to dart back if anything ended up going wrong.

"Hello?" I called out as I walked through the front door. I'd seen this segment in horror movies and played out the actions in my head. When the man bursts out, I would make for the door or find the sharpest and hardest object around me, and for the love of all things holy, I wouldn't scream!

"Yeah, can I help you?" an oddly calm voice from behind the counter spoke.

That was underwhelming, I thought to myself.

"I... I, uhh, I need to get out of this storm. Any idea where I can rest up for the night? I'm on my way to Lacoy National Park. Past there, actually," I said.

He stood up from behind the counter. A normal black hoodie, a normal pair of blue jeans, a normal person, just like me. "Yeah, man, there's a motel not more than a mile up on the right. They always got room. Not the nicest place to stay, but beats being out in this shit. You need anything while you're here?" he said.

I looked around trying to figure if there was anything I could buy, just to be polite in return for the advice. It hit me. Gas!

I hadn't filled my tank since I left my grandfather's. It's a miracle I hadn't stranded myself on the side of the road yet.

"Just a full tank, please, if you don't mind. Say about fifty dollars on, uh, pump one," I said, peering back out at my location under the overhang.

"Sure. You got it, brotha."

Running back to the truck I felt the panging of the rain mixed with the cold air. It hurt the exposed parts of my skin. At this rate the roads would be covered in black ice by the morning. *Good thing my four-wheel drive gave out over a year ago*, I thought, kicking my back tire as I filled the tank.

Pulling out of the station, I waved to the attendant and started on my way. He was right. Not more than a mile up on the right I saw the lights. A dainty and slightly crooked, almost cliché display. "Always Vacancies" shone in bright red letters. Hey, at least they were honest. I never thought to ask that guy how the hell they stay in business out here. Then again, it was the middle of the night. Never mind the fact that I didn't have a clue where I was; for all I knew an entire city was hiding itself just another mile up the road.

"Lacoy Motel Office" read the sign on the front door. The building itself looked as old as the trees that hung over its tight brick walls. Stained glass lined the outside, bubbled with the dangling raindrops that made their connection.

Parking under the overhang, same as I had at the gas station, I began to feel grateful of these businesses and their accommodations for this storm. I got out of my truck and almost expected a valet to come and take my keys. For a motel they had a fairly decent entrance. Red carpet lined the floors surrounded by gold-colored bars, and a similarly red overhang curled above my head. I could see the desk from the door outside. The receptionist was looking off at a TV overhead, filing her nails as she awaited my unexpected arrival.

I pulled the door softly so as not to startle the woman working the desk. To no avail she jumped from her seat and fixed her shirt, standing stiff as a board with a smile more artificial than the cartoon characters on the screen above her head. She was a fairly pretty woman. Blonde hair ran off her head and perfectly coated her shoulders. Her slender frame was attractive and intimidating as I fixed my clothes while approaching her, and near perfect teeth added to the suspense of her smile.

"Hello. Is it too late to get a room for the night? Definitely trying to get out of this storm," I said.

Without a moment's notice, the strangest display of lighting and music fazed in from the background. Men and women piled in from behind the wall of the counter, all sporting the same uniform as the front desk agent.

"First timer! First timer! First timer!" they chanted as they walked around me. One of them flicked the lights on at the bar in the corner of the lobby, standing at attention with a glass in one hand and a towel draped over his shoulder. Another stood at the door behind me, ready to open at any second. The rest were rumbling about doing anything they could to act like they were working rather than whatever they were doing moments before I arrived.

The receptionist had an embarrassed look on, as if she knew my presence had startled everyone to attention.

"Why, hello, sir! Oh! Is it raining out there? I can definitely get you any room you desire. We are only booked in three of our fourteen offerings! Would you like to see our room catalog?" she said, her voice less genuine than the people who had been playing cards and taking a nap just before I walked in.

Didn't notice the storm, though? No wonder she didn't expect me, either. Man, these people definitely were out of it.

Normally, going to a motel was a last resort for me. Like a blind date, choosing to go just anywhere for the hell of it was more than a gamble, yet there I was. I thought my town was small; I couldn't believe how a place like that stayed in business, so far from any main attraction, and so hidden unless you stumble upon it like I did.

"We are actually having a BOGO deal. If you select one of our twin rooms for the night you can stay for two nights at the price of one!" she said, customer service tone and all.

"I actually only need one night. But if those are the cheapest, I'll take it," I replied.

"You never know when you'll need to return. I'll keep you in the system, anyway."

I handed her my license, and she punched my name in the bulky box computer, a tan dinosaur of a machine. I expected half my stay would be waiting for her system to load, but not a minute later she slanted her head up. "All set! I'll show you to your room now."

We turned back for the door, and I remembered I always leave a small duffel with some items in case I stay the night at Aaron's unexpectedly. I cheered myself for the ingenuity and ran off to my truck, excusing myself on our route to my room.

I swung the bag over my shoulder, grabbed what was left of my flask, and tucked it in my back pocket. Away we went down what resembled an outside corridor. The red overhang swept over the entire perimeter of the motel. It was actually pretty impressive. We reached the room moments later.

"Here you are, Mr. Alec! I hope you enjoy your stay. One on the telephone will bring me to your room in moments if you have any problems! Have a good night now!" she said, starting back to the main office.

I tore my clothes from my body, swung them over the rail of the bathroom, and flailed myself onto the bed. For a motel in the middle of nowhere, again, I was impressed—a bed that didn't mimic the bricks that lay around the foundation of the building, and blankets that weren't ridden with more stains than my father's work clothes. The only downside was the lack of a television, which, although didn't mean much, gave me less of an opportunity to escape my thoughts. Thankfully I was buzzed enough to sleep it off and probably get into a dream or two within ten minutes of putting my head down.

I *clicked* off the lamp at my bedside and turned facing the window. The rain was still heavy and deep. Drops were falling, millions more than the naked eye could count. I focused on the heavy taps that the window felt. The next day would be heavier than this if I found what I was looking for. I wondered what might lie in my grandfather's old cabin. Would I find clothes, a picture, anything to make me see what my family had hidden from me for so long?

As my eyes started to dwindle, I was startled by the tap of something stronger than rain on the window before me. I could barely see, but a silhouette shown through the curtains—a large black brooding figure. A coat seemed to hang over its head. I tried to calm myself and remember that there were other people staying here.

I got up and approached the door, but when I glanced up at the window again, the figure was gone. I clasped the handle and rapidly swung the door open, looking out into the rain. I couldn't see more than ten yards, but it was enough to know whatever was there was gone now. I reminded myself that I was a young man, that I wasn't small, that I could hold my own—these were themes of my techniques to not freak out. Inside I was as small and fragile as an ant lost outside of its mound, but I looked in the mirror before me, blamed the drink for my hallucination, and headed back to bed.

I was able to get to sleep fairly quickly after what happened, but I had a dream way worse than the figure that perplexed me outside the window.

I was lying in the same bed in the same room, but the lights were now bright—brighter than any lights should be in any room for ideal comfort. I could barely see in front of me due to the glare, and then suddenly I heard the hounding *woof* of a dog, and the lights faded instantly.

Leaping to my feet, I looked around the room but was only met with the monochrome objects that lay before me. Moonlight shone on the corner of the dresser and illuminated the plastic wall of the shower, soaked in the golden handle of the door. The barking continued constantly: a dog standing right outside my door.

Swinging the door open, I met the dog in the middle of the street, looking right at me, telling me something, making me aware of its presence. I knew this dog. I knew what it was doing. It was making me know. It was making me aware. It was warning me of—

Honk honk went the horn of a truck, identical to mine, equal in color but in nicer condition. I only saw it in a snap, piercing through the rain, barreling through the street, and swiping through the dog as easily as it stole the wind from its place in the world.

I tried to turn my face, but I couldn't. It was staring back at me, making me know, making me aware. The dog lay whimpering, looking me in the eyes and breathing in fast and heavy sniffs. Its breathing ceased, and I turned away heading back into my room.

Beep! Beep! Beep! The alarm sounded louder than the horn of the truck barreling through the street. I leapt to my feet and started for the door. The drink definitely hit me harder today. The nightmare was one I had many times. The only thing that changed was the setting. Always my truck, always that damned dog haunting me.

I folded backward, cracking my back and yawning simultaneously. The sun was finally out. I looked outside, and it was drier than the desert in the middle of July. Not a stain or a puddle was in sight to trace the rain that had come the night before.

Just as I had done when I got home two nights before, I left my truck in a place that gave away my intoxication. Half of the bed crushed the bushes that once laid delicately along the edge of the driveway. I was embarrassed and made my way to the motel so I could be on my way.

As I approached the office to return my key, her voice shouted from behind me, "Mr. Alec, sir, are you going to be checking out now?"

I swung around to see her pacing rapidly toward me. Her purple velvet pajamas highlighted the fuzzy slippers she was sporting below. Ignoring her clothes because I myself wasn't a stickler for professionalism, I tossed the keys to her. "Thank you for your help. Unfortunately, I gotta go now," I said, more worried than rude.

"Mr. Alec. Not to be blunt, don't mind my impression, but you look as though you wouldn't mind a cup of coffee and some breakfast," she said.

Not to be rude myself, but a very good looking girl asking me to breakfast—even in purple pajamas—was sure to grab my attention. Whether she had a maniacal stare when she was faking her work tone and worked at a motel in the middle of nowhere or not, she was right. I followed her as she paced by me, her eyes locked on mine until her head turned.

"Give me one minute, Mr. Alec. Let me change into my day clothes. I'll meet you just inside the lobby," she said.

"You can just call me Alec!" I said as she disappeared into her room.

Sticking her head back out the door she said, "Oookay, Mr. Alec," and slipped in with a smile.

The first two people I met while out in those woods were pretty hospitable. I felt much more comfortable after meeting the desk agent, though, even if I didn't know her name yet. It wasn't like my grandfather's house was going anywhere. I was in a hurry to get out of town, but I had a few minutes to spare and talk to an attractive lonely woman in the middle of nowhere.

The lobby looked just as cliché in the daylight, with the minor difference of the sunlight spilling in. Small floating dust mites made their way left to right through the waves of sun that poured through the stained-glass windows. They painted their reflections multiple colors as they landed on different objects throughout the room.

The characters that were there the night before were still at their posts, as if they didn't sleep, or as if they were robots. "Hello, Mr. Alec," the doorman said as he led me through to the counter. At the bar still stood the same employee as well, his hands still on a glass the same as the one he clutched the night before. There was an uncanniness in the air; an undeniably odd atmosphere was present there. I just decided to let it go and continued.

"Okay, I'm starving. Let's eat!" she said, bursting in through the door behind me back in her uniform, same as the night before.

I followed her down a hallway on the side of the lobby into a large but empty dining area. I looked to her. "You know, I'm a pretty good cook."

"Oh, really? Well, it's a good thing you're our guest, because we already have the food prepared for you, Alec," she followed with a smirk.

"Good morning, Gabriella!" a man said coming through the door of the kitchen. "Oh, you must be our lovely guest! Thank you so much for staying with us today!" he said, laying a platter in front of me: a lavish set of fresh fruits, the instant smell of perfectly crisped bacon and linked sausages, complemented with the aroma of warm baked biscuits.

"Thank you, sir!" she replied.

"Uhh… yeah, thank you, sir!" I followed.

"Please, enjoy. If you need anything else, come ring the bell!" he replied, pointing to the shiny golden bell that sat atop the kitchen window at the edge of the room.

I was embarrassed. I felt more like I was at a new friend's house than a motel, nor did I expect that motels had continental breakfast. Either way, I didn't mind. I put my hands to work, and my mouth was the judge. Crisp and tender bites went down smoothly, and after the first few bites I remembered I hadn't even eaten since the funeral the day before.

I must've filled my plate three times before I was done. Truth be told the embarrassment trumped my fullness and I would've eaten more had it been Aaron or my parents sitting at the other end of the table instead of such a pretty girl.

"I know how cliché this sounds, but you're not from around here, are you?" she asked.

"Not too far, actually. Only a few hours east. My grandfather has a house just past Lacoy. I was on my way there, and then I needed somewhere to crash through the storm," I replied.

"Well, you've come right to the heart of the town!" she said. "We're right in the middle of the up and the down. As we call it here, anyway," she let out with a chuckle.

"The 'up and the down'?" I asked.

"Listen, honey, I know you're here to see your family. Every-one passes through here to visit family; that's just how it is. At least if you're up, then you can go to the down, but if you're down, you can't really go to the up. So, what do you do? Tell me about yourself!" she asked.

I didn't understand. "What do you mean they can't?"

"Well, it's not that important since you're passing through from the east, but if you're up then you're *really* up—like privilege, prestige, all that good stuff—and if you're down, you probably don't have the status to go up. So, people who are up can visit people who are down, and down on their luck, but people who are down can only go so far as here, honestly, and meet people in the middle if they want," she explained.

"No offense, but I don't really follow your logic. That's a pretty weird setup. Is there, like, a border wall or something?" I asked.

"Kind've. I don't know. Well anyway, you're going to see your grandpa, *right*?" she asked.

"Not really. He lives east of here now in the same town as me. Seeing how this town works I don't blame him, honestly. No offense. I'm passing through to grab some things of his from his old house and bring them back to him," I added.

She ate as gracefully as a deer nestled by a brook; as calmly as a songbird landing on a flower. I was more comforted by her presence than attracted by her looks. For the first time since I ran off, I felt like I was around someone trustworthy enough to listen, but I couldn't be so naive. I kept my guard up but was thankful for the hospitality all the same.

"Look, I apologize greatly for my rudeness, but I have to get going. My grandfather is expecting a lot of this stuff to be back before the end of the day today. So, I'd be better off getting an early start," I said.

"As you wish. If you do find yourself wanting to return, you did purchase the room with a BOGO deal. Remember?" she asked, followed with another huge smile. This time, though, it didn't look or feel artificial or maniacal. It was calmer and more relaxing than before.

I stood from the table. "Again, thank you so much for this! Really hit the spot, I swear." And I started back down the hallway. She was following right behind me; I could hear her soft steps tracing mine as I approached the exit. When I got to my truck, I turned the key to get going, and nothing happened.

Not a single noise, not a single turn. The motor was more than dead—it was lifeless. The truck was more than stuck, it was glued—glued to this very spot in the earth. Unfortunately, it didn't sound like any years of my work at my father's shop would teach me how to fix that break down.

I looked up at her; she was smiling at me. I gave it another turn and could not even hear the sound of the fuel pump engaging. The tiniest peep was silenced. A bead of rain through the broken gasket plopping on the floor and the turn of the decade old key was all I could hear.

I jumped down from the truck. "Well, it looks like I may be staying that extra night," I said.

"Nonsense. I have a car. I can take you wherever you need to go," she said.

"No, that's okay. I can just call for a—" No service. Not a single bar to connect me back to the world I drove over here from. The panic started to set in. My phone was close to dying— solely saved by the fact that I hadn't opened it in twenty-four hours, but it didn't matter anyway.

"I guess you have no choice now. I'll be right back. Give me five minutes!" she said.

Chapter 5

I felt the air at the back of my neck making the hairs stand firm. Day by day it was getting closer to winter. The squeak and drag of a fence pulling across the pavement grabbed my attention. There she was, pulling the fence open to get her car out from the garage. As she approached me, smile and all, I felt bad that I wasn't more appreciative of her help, but I wanted to go about the drive on my own.

I thanked her for her hospitality. "You don't need to run the desk today?" I asked.

"No way; today's my day off. Pretty lucky for us, actually!" she replied.

The car smelt delightful. A silky lavender oozed from the air conditioner and pampered my nose upon entering. A smell much nicer than the damp and dusty undertones my truck had to offer. An instant calm was pulled over me. Gabriella looked to me and smiled.

It was odd to me. At least she made me realize it. When I was a young man, it was exciting meeting someone new—a female, I mean. She was pretty, and very hospitable at that. When I first met her, she had no clue of my past. No idea what I had done right or wrong or how messed up my family was. She didn't even know what I liked or disliked. Meeting a new person was like starting a new life. But it's like my grandfather said. The more we go on, the more we hold inside until it all just spills over in front of everyone.

As excited as I was in that moment, I was also brought back to the stark reality that we all are who we are in this world. We can't escape who we are in new people. We can, though, find people who like us just the way we are. Either way, it was nice to be around someone new in a different place. For a brief moment I almost felt relieved, then I remembered why I was there, and it all came back to me.

"So, you want to go just past Lacoy National Park? What then?"

"Well, my grandfather said it's going to be the first access road after the park sign. If we follow it for a few miles we should come up on the house. I'm pretty sure it's the only one out here. You don't have to come inside, though; in case there's someone living in there I don't want to get you caught in a mess," I added.

She smiled, looked back toward the road, and started to the house. "That's very nice of you, Alec. You're a very nice man," she said.

I wouldn't consider myself overly nice by any means. I always tried my best to understand people and where they were coming from. It's what I got from my father. There were countless times when people couldn't pay their bills at the shop. They pleaded and explained that they couldn't get to work to pay him if they didn't have their car back. My father always complied, and his heart won over his stern stature.

Even when I would ask him why he accepted he would always say, "We are all going through it, Alec. We are either at the end of it, the beginning, or stuck right in the middle. When you're in it, you know what it's like when someone gives you a push. As cliché as it may sound, don't stop pushing other people," he would say.

As we drove further and further from the motel, the air seemed to grow thicker. The sun sat tighter behind the clouds and was more unforgiving than before. It might have been a compilation of my building nerves and the uncertainty of what I would find, but enough to provide a change in atmosphere.

Just at the right moment, when the silence grew too much to bear, she asked, "You're nervous about something. Right? I don't know everything about everyone, but I can sense when a person should start talking more and think less."

"I'm not exactly going here for what I said I was," I replied, figuring honesty and a fresh set of ears might help to soothe my distress.

"Okay… Well, I'm all ears. If you want to talk, I will listen; won't even reply if you don't want," she said.

I thought about where exactly to start. There I was, being excited about meeting a new, pretty girl. Telling her my brother murdered my uncle and I'm chasing after his ghost wouldn't have been the best way to continue down this path. Quite frankly, I had no other way to put it, and to my delight she really wasn't the judging type, so I continued.

"Years ago, my older brother… I guess… I guess he accidentally killed my uncle. I know that's super aggressive to say right off, and I'm sorry. Anyway, he ran away to this house, and I never knew about it—I'm not even supposed… not even supposed to be here. This is the last place he came, though, and my family doesn't know I'm here, but I need to know—need to know if there is anything here I can use to learn about him," I said, my voice shaking.

After a brief pause, she replied without any change of expression.

"Wow. I am really sorry about that, Alec. Well, is he still here? I mean, does he live there or something?" she asked.

I was surprised by her reaction, half expecting a gasp and for her to turn around and take me back to the motel, saying she wanted me to find another ride.

"No. My family told me he died in an accident on his way back to our town. He's been dead for eighteen years now." Her eyes peered forward in disbelief. She didn't seem scared as much as confused to how she should reply. I figured I would save her from an awkward blunder. "But hey, it's over now. I just have some free time, and figured I'd come check it out is all," I added.

"Alec, I know you're not going to believe me—it was long ago when this happened—but I do remember. I know what happened to your brother."

"You *know* about my brother?" I asked, fingers clenching and shoulders tense.

"I never knew him, obviously, but I was there when it happened. At least, I think I was. In this town, around this motel, there was only one accident that happened. This was in the dead center of July. It was so hot that the pavement burned my bare feet. I was sitting in the grass lying under the sun. All of a sudden, I heard the squeal of brakes on the road before me. When I got up to look it all happened so fast. There was a truck wedged between two trees, so tight that they couldn't get it out with a tow truck or trailer or anything."

"How do you know that was my brother? Like, how do you really know?"

"I will never forget for the remainder of my life. David Godfrey was his name. If that's your brother, then yes, that's the same person who I'm talking about. I'll never forget his name," she said.

I stared into the dashboard ahead of me. The calming smell was the only thing holding back a panic attack. I thought of a slew of questions to ask her but opted to just sit in silence for the rest of the ride.

I thought more about my conscience than about the things she had said. What made a family; what made brothers, brothers? What made me actually drive all the way out here and actually care, actually give a shit about this guy who did nothing for my family and killed his own uncle?

Family is about belonging, about memories, about sharing a place in each other's heart. This boy, this man—whoever he was—he wasn't in my memory; he wasn't in my heart. I twisted and grappled with the idea of subconsciously being so worried and engrained in this and just turning back out of sheer stupidity.

He and I had never shared a room, never passed the football in the backyard, never laughed together, smiled, cried, fought... nothing. Never anything at all.

My arms were moving inside of me, but I held myself back. I was biting my tongue, screaming behind closed lips.

Out of panic, sheer complete panic, I punched the dashboard in front of me. I punched it, and I screamed, and I screamed over and over, louder and louder. I let it all out.

Why did no one let me see him? Why did I care so much? What in the world brought me out here in search of anything? Nothing would bring him back; nothing ever would.

I looked to my side apologetically without a single word. I began to cry, softly and silently, but it wasn't enough to hide it from her.

She didn't say anything else for the remainder of our travels. We got to the access road and just looked for the house, saying a word here and there to call out what looked like a mailbox but wasn't, what might've been but didn't seem to be. Finally, I saw it: a break in the forest and a mailbox sitting slant on the edge of the road. There was no doubt in my mind that was the house, and I could feel it even before seeing the structure.

I felt twitching in my fingers and shock pulsing in the backs of my thighs. That was pure adrenaline ripping through my bloodstream, a feeling that nothing could match. Both fright and fury entangled me from head to toe. My body was once again proving to me that I couldn't understand. Couldn't understand why I even cared.

As we pulled down the long dirt driveway, the car bustled and rolled left and right, dipping in the divots back and forth as we continued.

When we finally reached the end of the road, we saw the house. Its structure was as simple and stern as my grandfather's personality, each piece of wood laid gently and meticulously in its original place. The setting, though, couldn't have been more opposing to what I know about him. I was so used to seeing him on the busiest street in my town. Although it was small, cars went up and down that main road all day and night. The house was him, but the surrounding was foreign to me, and in turn felt foreign to him too. Too isolated and alone for comfort.

No overgrown moss lined the windows and crept up the sides of the house. Not a single blade of grass was high enough to seem uncut. I was growing wary of the possibility that someone did inhabit this house, but there were no cars in the driveway.

I got out of the car and started toward the house slowly, cautious of anyone coming out the front door with a gun pointed in my direction. I searched around the front for the turtle. Stepping carefully through the grass, I spotted the garden statue on the deck, just off the front step. An antique plastic turtle, sporting a purple bandanna and a cartoon smile.

I picked the turtle up and flipped it on its back, turning the stomach open to grab the key. I couldn't believe it: After eighteen years, it was still there. Even if someone was living here, they hadn't thought to change the spot of the original owner's key.

I took my first step up to the house and turned back to the car.

She was sitting, smiling at me, and I felt like she was awaiting my permission.

I didn't think she would accept so I offered. "You coming?" I shouted, and with that she instantly cut the engine off and jumped out of the car.

Excitement and fear waged war inside of me, each step feeling equally hard to take as it was to resist.

I put the key to the door and looked to her. "Are you ready?" she asked. I wasn't, honestly. An uneasy flood of emotion was ruining any confidence I had for entering the house, and I had no clue what I would find. I imagined bottles emptied and riddled across the floor, or clothes and items that belonged to David all over the place. When I turned the key and swung the door open, nothing matched my anticipation.

Without a single item out of place, and not a single mess to examine, I was in awe of the cleanliness of this place. What my grandfather had prepared me for to be a nightmare of a structure was merely another house on another street, like someone had left it just minutes before.

All the angst, fear, and worry was replaced with confusion. How would it have been possible that the last inhabitant of that house was my brother eighteen years earlier? I stepped further in to look around but was careful that there may be someone around any corner.

What stood out to me the most was the balcony overlooking the entire house that stood right above the main living area. Although meticulous, the tiny structure was too small to contain many rooms. Wooden beams lined the ceiling and could be jumped to from the railing of the balcony. I wondered if my grandfather ever tried, maybe broke a bone on a missed attempt even.

I ran up the side of the steps and presented myself in front of her from the top, with my arms wide and a smile even broader. She looked up to me and laughed. The shock was eternal. It was carrying me through my tour. There was no bathroom; I could see the outhouse from the window on the balcony. There were two twin beds that faced each other, again part of this balcony that spanned much further back into the house than I had imagined from the ground floor.

Not a full kitchen, either. There was a black kettle large as it was wide. It was brimming with char from previous nights of boiling stew, probably made from my grandfather's catch of the day while hunting with his father in the woods that swallowed the house's perimeter.

Nothing of David, though. Not a scrap of clothing torn on the floor, not an empty bottle that he drained before leaving. There wasn't a trace. My adrenaline slowed, and I walked down the stairs to the living area, sitting on the couch. I peered around the room, happy that I was there but obviously unfulfilled. I looked up. There was a TV with a VHS on its head. Definitely not something that my "live off the land" grandfather would have had. I shot up and pressed the button at the front of the VHS. He must've brought this with him when he used to come out here. There had to have been other occasions where he ventured out to this house. Maybe David used to bring girls here. Maybe he used to have parties just like me.

When I hit the eject button, a VHS tape presented itself with a label that read, "DAVID'S FOURTH BIRTHDAY!" I froze in panic; again, excitement engulfed in a flame of terror. The pit of my stomach was the new landlord for my heart, and when I finally mustered the ability to shake the feeling, back in it went.

I turned on the TV, upped the volume, and sat with Gabriella on the couch across the way. She hadn't said a word since I got there. She just looked to me and smiled, all the while taking in what it was, understanding what I was doing. I appreciated her presence; it was something more than comforting. I trusted her without knowing her, but I was more than okay with that.

The screen shuttered, and on it went. I would never forget a single moment. It was short, but my eyes were glued to the screen for the entirety of the video. There my father was, younger and fresher than I had ever seen him. His eyes were lightened.

David was so small. He was nothing yet, just a child. Even at four years old he didn't have any life behind him.

Seeing him so preciously, barely even having the mouth to take a bite of cake or to run in a straight line, it pained me to see him like this. I didn't care if I didn't understand who he was to me; I could see who he was to my father.

"They were so happy before—before he grew older and ruined it all for them," I said bluntly, faster than I regretted it.

"Alec. Come on. I'm assuming your brother wasn't a perfect person, if that's what you mean. Whatever he did is behind him, though. He paid the ultimate price for his actions. I'm sure your parents miss him more than they were mad at him. Don't you agree?"

She was right. "But what if he finally did something that couldn't be forgiven?" I asked.

"Sometimes forgiving others is the best way to find peace, Alec. I'm sure your parents forgave him," she said.

"My father has dedicated his life to them—to my uncle's family—so much that he's barely a part of mine."

"I'm sorry, Alec. But you know, sometimes you really do have to forget the past, and it's the only way to enlarge the future. Now that you know what happened to your family, maybe you can help your dad. Maybe he's right there, in the middle of it, and he needs a push even though he's been there pushing everyone else, like you said," she replied.

Again, she was right. I couldn't respond, but I also couldn't disagree. Her words cut deep. My father wasn't perfect. He never was. But holding on to what I thought I lost in him didn't bring back the time we already missed.

I rose from the couch and chose to survey the rest of the house, letting the video play in a circuit again and again, listening to David laughing and my father and mother talking to each other. The feeling brought me peace. It made me understand forgiveness. I wasn't mad at my family; I was misunderstood. I got to the top of the stairs and started shuffling through the drawers. All were empty except one. I reached in and grabbed a varsity coat that had sat at the bottom of the dresser. A startling logo was stitched into the back of it. Brooding white letters lined the black cloth that I had in my hands. "Godfrey" was stitched into the left shoulder. I was stunned. He had left something behind. In this house, where he hid, he left it behind. That jacket was with him. It held all his regret, all his anger, his maltreatment of others, his mistakes.

Leaving that jacket behind meant one of two things to him. Either he was going to start a new life, or there was no going back from the one he already had. When he died that day, he had one thing in mind. Maybe he was going to see my parents, or maybe he was just going.

I slipped my arm into the first side and my other into the next. I walked to the mirror by the bedside and zipped it up half way.

I couldn't believe it—a perfect fit.

Chapter 6

——

As I walked down the steps, my shoulders cocked and head held high, I was surprised to see Gabriella staring back at me without a smile. Her joyful and happy prose was quickly replaced with a cold and confused stare, like I just did something wrong. I stared back at her, ignoring the look. "I'm ready to go."

I took the VHS tape from the television and started for the door, turning to take one look back at the house. Looking up at the balcony, I envisioned David, my grandfather, and his father all standing on that same spot. I was happy I got to witness it too.

The feeling the jacket gave off entranced me wholly. I wondered who it had been worn by apart from my brother. Maybe the strongest people around shared that patch. I wondered how many times he had felt free and how many times he felt powerful wearing that patch. I also thought of how many times he hurt people wearing it—how many times he made my parents sad and worried. Maybe that was the jacket he wore when he killed my uncle.

Either way, I came for anything I could have that reminded me of him. This was what I needed, and I was ready to go back now.

"Are you... Are you sure you want to keep that, Alec?" she asked. "Wouldn't it be better to just leave it here?"

"I'd like to think he wanted me to keep this," I said in a sharp tone. "Now let's go, so I can figure out how to get the hell out of here."

She looked to the ground and started out the door before me. I didn't take a single breath before looking up and seeing him.

An old man who couldn't have been less than eighty years old. His camouflage overalls were tucked down into his knee-high boots. He had a line of fish tied together over his right shoulder and a pole over the other.

A year's grown beard, grayer than the surface of the moon, suspended down to the top of his chest. His hair was, although short, wilder and more misguided than his beard, with strands flying in all sorts of directions. Yes, no doubt I knew he had been inhabiting this place for the last little while.

"Sir. I know what you're going to say... but please—" I started.

"Just take that jacket off. Unless you're going to take every-thing I have too," he started.

I looked down in confusion and over to Gabriella who defi-nitely knew what he meant. Her face was as silent as it was clear. "Alec. That jacket. Those people. It's not as clear as you think," she started.

He walked past me with a limp that lowered his right side each step he took. "Lunch will be ready in an hour if you want it. If not, then get the hell off my property," he said.

My face grew stern. I clenched my fists and felt a fire in my heart raging wildly. Who the hell was this man telling me to get off *his* property? *His* house? I turned to shout at him, but Gabriella grabbed my shoulder. "Alec. Don't. No one has lived here in eighteen years. This house is nothing more than a cabin in the woods. He didn't steal anything from you. He's so old he'll probably be gone soon, anyway. Why punish him? Where would he go, anyway?" she asked.

I already had what I wanted—what I needed. But why didn't he act surprised to see us—to see me? I gave myself a few seconds to brush away my anger.

"Hey, old man. What're you doing here? How come you didn't care to see people here?" I asked.

He turned and put his arm down on the old wooden chair to the right of the door. He fell back into the seat and let out a low groan and sigh. Grabbing a handkerchief from the pocket of his overalls, he let out a nasty cough and wiped the side of his mouth. "Son, I've lived here forever. Do you think I give a shit to see a few kids walking out the front door, one of them wearing some petty gang jacket that belonged to some kid who drove off and died at the end of the road? I won't be here for much longer. Now, you want some lunch, or do you want to get the fuck off my lawn?"

I stood back in disbelief. My eyes widened, and my fists that were once clenched were shaking in shock. Who did this guy think he was? What was I going to do, fight an old man? Starting back toward the car, I trudged off angrily until he started, "Hey, kid! Kids! Get back here. Come on, I don't get much company, anyway. Just spend an hour or so." A complete shift of attitude. I didn't know where his anger came from, but his newfound generosity was even more of a mystery.

"Yeah, I think I'm all set. Thanks, though," I said.

"I've lived in these woods for years, kid. And based on that jacket you're wearing, I know exactly who it is you were here to see. I was here the day he died. Do you want to know what he said to me before it happened?" he asked.

I didn't believe him. How would he have known about this jacket, though, or "that night" as he said? I turned to Gabriella, and she smiled. "Maybe this is exactly what you need. For closure, Alec." She looked happy. "I'll go back to the motel. I'll be back in an hour or so to come pick you up! I can see if I can get some help for your truck too. All right?" she continued.

"Thank you. I can't explain how to repay you, but I promise—"

"Save it, Alec. I'm more than happy to help. I swear," she replied, cutting me off in the nicest possible way.

That was all so random. First the house's condition, then the jacket. Then all of a sudden, some random old man appears claiming to know my brother's fate. The air was still cold and damp. My lungs felt clogged and my vision hazy. Almost like a dream, but there I was standing before him. That man probably had all the answers to what I was looking for. For a minute it just seemed too good to be true.

I smiled in embarrassment at how angry I had just been and looked down to my feet. "Sure, sir. I'd love to take you up on that offer," I said. With that I went back toward the house and sat in the matching wooden chair at the other side of the door.

"I know I came off rude," he started, followed by another cough and a wipe of his handkerchief. There was blood this time. "I didn't know if you'd come, if anyone would come. Eighteen years I sat with the things that that kid told me, waiting for his family to come by and ask about him. Eighteen years later no one said anything. No wonder the kid was going off the deep end," he said.

"You blame me? I wasn't even alive! My parents, my grandparents—I don't know what to say when it comes to them, but me... I don't know," I said.

"I'm not blaming anyone, son. Especially not some kid not even alive to know the difference. I don't remember everything he told me, but he was broken. For a long time he was broken. Always tried to put the pieces back together. I was here with him for about three weeks before he finally left. He was paranoid, spread too thin," he explained.

And with that he got up and headed into the house. He laid the fish down on the table and pulled a knife from his right hip.

"You wanna watch this, kid?" he asked.

I guess I never knew how to clean a catch, nor did I really care. As I would've said to my grandfather, though, it was worth watching to make the guy feel good; besides, he was going to tell me just about everything I wanted to know.

"Sure. Why not?" I replied.

I couldn't believe how much actually went into that process. He talked about washing the slime, laying it out with a certain end facing away from him, even cutting just shallow enough that you don't touch the organs. Who would've known that something that intricate, that small, had to be treated with such care and thought?

It puzzled me why people spend so much time on the smallest things and then act like some things in their life are beyond capable of being repaired. My father spent hours and hours in that shop day after day, nights on end. He would sometimes work twenty-four hours straight, and in the morning we'd find him passed out in the front seat of a car he was working on.

He worked so hard to provide, so hard to fix the broken pieces of what he thought he had caused. He never spent that amount of time fixing David or what he could've been. I wondered if that was why he lived with so much regret.

My father said work was the only place where you wouldn't make mistakes so long as you did your job. His job was to fix what he could handle, to fix something he knew the pieces to.

When the old man finished preparing the fish, he threw them into the pot, added some chopped vegetables, and sat back in a frail wooden chair by the kitchen counter. He coughed again and followed it with a slow groan that caused me to ask, "Do you know what's wrong with you?"

"Just time, son. Death works on a clock. It comes for us all. I've already been gone a while. People stopped speaking my name far before I got sick. By that time, I'd already been dead," he replied. "Back to your brother. I know he did a lot of it to himself, but I'll never forget what he told me right before he walked off that porch," he started.

"And what was that?" I returned.

"When he walked onto those steps the night he arrived, I already knew he was dead, just like me. And when he started off these steps and back to his truck, he knew it too. He looked at me, and I asked where his life would take him next. He looked back and said there wasn't anywhere else for it to go. When I walked back inside and saw that jacket hung up on the base of the stairs by the fire, I knew he gave up," he said.

The loneliness and isolation that grew inside of this house was as apparent as the forest that engulfed it.

"This jacket. I know it belonged to him, but who did he belong to?" I asked.

"Nothing more than a group of half-wits scrumming around taking other people's things and poking their noses where it didn't belong. Started with some man, more than a man by the way he possessed those people. He had some ideology, embracing your dark side or some horse shit like that. When he hooked people in, people like your brother, they were as good as gone. Your brother's fate wasn't so unique, you know," he added. "Forget about that, though, kid. Let's eat. Okay? After you try my famous fish stew then I'll let you keep asking me whatever you want," he finished.

He placed the bowl down in front of me. The aroma—produced by a marriage of celery, carrots, potatoes, and the heavy cream he added as a last touch—presented itself in front of me. A fresh fish chowder—I hadn't had a bowl of this in years. At the time, thinking I was in my grandfather's old house, eating a bowl of chowder similar to the one he used to make for me, was weird. A relic it was, how appropriate to have a meal that was that memorable in his house. When I looked up to ask the man my next question, I was met with a less-than-comforting stare.

"What is it?" I asked. "It looks amazing, just like my grandpa used to do back when he was able to cook more often. Nowadays he just kind of moseys around. Now that my grandmother died, I bet it'll be even worse," I added.

"She died, huh?" He looked to me in disbelief. "She was a good woman," he said.

"What?" I replied, thinking I hadn't heard him right.

"Oh, I, uh—I said she must've been a really good woman. If your grandfather is going to change that much without her.

Their love must've really meant something," he said, hurling the joke off with embarrassed and forced laughter. "Anyway, your grandfather must be a good man then, making a stew like mine. That isn't what I'm after, though. I want to tell you a story, if you have no more questions for me," he said.

Taking my first bite of his stew, I couldn't believe how amazing the fish tasted when cut that fresh. That wasn't like my grandfather's stew; that was even better. The creamy broth, the crunchy taste of celery—it was enough to distract me from the man's question, buy me some time to think of an answer. *Oh, what the hell, why not listen to a story? Old people love to tell stories.*

"Yes, sir. Let's hear it," I replied.

"Okay, perfect," he said, pushing his bowl away from him and leaning back in his chair. He pulled a long black pipe to his mouth and lit the end. I knew a man like him.

After puckering his lips on its pointed end, he let out a puff of smoke, cleared his throat, and told me this story:

There was a man and a woman. They were entranced by their love for each other. He said love drowned them like a wave sweeping them with its undertow, deeper as it sailed like an underwater ship. They spent years together, countless moons. They laid under infinite amounts of stars. The best of friends, the feeblest of enemies. One day the woman fell very ill. They had no cure for what she had, couldn't even tell the man what it was. This was back in a day where medicine wasn't so advanced. Even the smartest and most renowned doctors couldn't save this woman, neither could they figure out what caught her. The man began to grow restless. He would spend his days by her bedside, praying to a god he forced himself to commit to. He grew tired of medicine and science and just sat looking to God, praying for an answer.

Then one day when he awoke, the opening of his eyes introduced him to the cease of her breath. He sat weeping and crying, looking down to her. He cursed God and himself and the doctors around. There was nothing they could do, and he couldn't believe his own hopelessness. The man chose to keep his bride by his side as long as he could. One day went by and then the next. When men approached his door, he was startled to find they hadn't come to take her from him, rather to tell him of a new medicine they developed. An experimental doctor was going door to door selling a pill that granted eternal life. Of course, there were side effects, and the possibility that it was all a lie. He then spoke of another pill, and when he looked at the man's wife, deceased and decayed, he knew he could do as he wished. He told the man that the other pill would bring his wife back from the dead, that she would awake in the morning and look just as she did before she died. It wasn't proven to take away the pain that she felt, but it would make her come back to him. The man without hesitation went to his wife and placed the pill between her lips, praying that it would make its way to her insides. He rushed the men off and went to sleep, and when he awoke in the morning, he couldn't believe what he was seeing. There she was, alive, open eyes, smiling her crooked smile just as he had admired for all those years. He looked to her with open embrace and hugged her as hard as he could.

When he hugged her, she began to cough, and the cough got worse and worse. He asked of her condition to which she had no idea of the state. She just said that she had woken up and had no recollection of her passing. He watched through the next few weeks as she wept and cried in pain. She sobbed from the same aches that she felt before her passing; she croaked for air at the same loss of breath that she had once felt. The man grew more than angry and went down to the lab where he knew the doctor worked.

He approached the man. Enraged and confused, he slammed the man's desk before him and asked, "Why would you give me this pill? My wife isn't any better than she was before she died. You didn't cure her, you just made her suffer even more," he said.

"I didn't choose anything, sir. I gave you exactly what you asked for. I gave her life back. I told you I couldn't guarantee her state, and you understood that. I can't take away her suffering. Life is sometimes full of suffering," he said. With that, he took another pill from his coat pocket. Strange as it was, the power that pill held was just as strong as the other. He explained to the man that if he gave his wife this pill, she would be returned to the state that she was in before he gave her the first. She would die.

The man went home and pondered his decision. He sat next to her all day, playing chess and reading to her, but at night he listened to her sobbing and croaking for air. The pattern repeated night after night until he couldn't understand how to handle it anymore. Her condition got worse and worse. She couldn't even eat at her lowest point; he felt that he was starving her. He looked to her one night and offered her the pill as a medicine just like any other. He really could not handle listening to her suffering, enduring her pain. He was mad at the man for doing this to him and mad at himself for the same reason.

When he awoke in the morning, he saw her; the opening of his eyes introduced him to the ceasing of her breath. When he saw her, though, he didn't feel the same pain as he did before. He didn't feel the same tyrannical anger toward God's actions as he did the first time. He was relieved—relieved that she was no longer weeping, that she no longer croaked for air. She looked more peaceful than she had in years before her death.

The man held services for her. He had his family and friends surrounding him, and they buried her, understood her passing, and left it at that. The man returned home and wasn't angry. He went to the lab and thanked the doctor for his understanding. He apologized to God for his anger and curses and ended his own mental suffering in his understanding of death.

My eyes were locked to my feet below me. I scratched my heels on the floor of the house. I didn't know if he was done or not, but I looked up to him to see him still looking into the wall of the house. He wasn't crying, but a well of tears shined around the bottom of his eyes, until one tear ran solemnly down his cheek, ending with a splat on the table below him.

"I—I don't understand, sir. This man brought her back to life, and then he killed her again?" I asked.

"Son. You just don't mess with the nature of life. Death isn't always a punishment. It isn't always God's way of taking something from us. Sometimes people have so much inside of them and so many things to hold on to that they would be better off to just let go. Death isn't always a punishment from every perspective," he said. "Sometimes death isn't a terrible thing. If you think about it, sometimes death teaches us—"

And I ended the sentence in unison with him, both of us looking up and locking eyes with each other, "Our most important lesson about life."

Chapter 7

The sun was beginning to set. We were sitting in silence at that point. After a few moments, headlights shone through the window passing along the walls. I looked out the window and back to the man once again.

"It isn't too late, son. We can never truly let go of the ones we love. It'll always be inside of you, from this point onward. You can always remember him for who he could've been, though. Might just help you realize who you ought to be," he said.

I got up; he still hadn't touched his food. He finished his pipe, stayed back in his seat, and looked up to the roof above him. I pulled the jacket off my back, each sleeve coming off much harder than how it slipped on. I placed the cassette on the table; he looked to it surprisingly as if it meant as much to him as it did to me. The second I placed it down, he grabbed it. Before I could ask him why, the door swung open, and she returned. Gabriella stood with a solemn smile, the headlights shining around her silhouette as she remained by the door.

"Are you ready, Alec?" she asked.

I looked back to him, smiling, and thanked him for the food. As I started toward the door, I swung around, taking one more look up at the balcony overlooking the entirety of the house.

On that ride back to the motel, when I seemingly got what I was looking for, I came to a realization right then and there. Life and death are way too similar. Death isn't just some black hole that awaits us. It isn't the ending of joy and the passage to a dimension filled with grief and disdain. Death is a passage to another life. It's just the second half of our story. Someone somewhere intended for death. It wasn't an accident that we all die at some point, it's just something that we must learn to understand.

I know the story was nothing more than folklore, but everyone who mourns has wished for the same pill at some point in their life. Everyone wishes in the first stage of grief to have that person back and forgets the pain and the suffering they endured when they were still alive. Maybe David was going through pain and suffering far worse than he is now. Maybe if my parents had a pill to bring him back, he would just remember what he did to our uncle and wish himself back to death. I hoped that somewhere, wherever he was among the stars, he was free from whatever pain he felt down here on earth.

I was young when the man told me this story. Free from grief and free from loss. I wonder what my parents felt—what fifty years of life does to a person internally. I wondered why people want to live and if others truly want to die. If people remember they were alive once they pass on, do they want to go back, or do they accept the release that they were inevitably made to be a part of?

"It's okay to ask, you know," I said.

"I just hope more than anything that you found what you were intending to, coming all the way out here. I know it's weird, some old guy living in your family's old house, but he probably doesn't have much time left. Maybe you could just leave it a secret from your family?" she asked.

I stayed silent. *Maybe I'd keep it secret.*

We passed by the motel, triggering my confusion. "What happened to my truck? Where did it go?"

"I called the local shop right down the street not more than a few hundred yards. They'll take care of it. It's going to be a lengthy fix, but I know the owner; he's a very nice man. I'm sure we can work something out for you," she said.

Her affirmation was refreshing. I wasn't nervous at all, and I was appreciative of her help. Being around her made me feel safe.

"So, what do you like to do? Around here it doesn't seem like there's much," I followed with a chuckle.

"I just work. I never really had a family; I've lived at this motel my whole life. I've never actually been out of this town, believe it or not. You know the saying 'ignorance is bliss,' right? I like to think this is the most beautiful corner of the universe, and it couldn't get much better than this," she said.

"So, you've never been out of the country, or even the state? Didn't your parents ever take you on vacations?" I followed.

"It's complicated, but since you so willingly spilled all your family trauma, I guess I will too. I never had a real mother and father. Everyone here at the motel raised me. From what they say one of the housekeeping maids found me out by the dumpster behind the motel one night, and the rest was history. They were my family when no one else was. So, I just worked here and now I manage everything. Sure, I've wanted to leave, but, like I said, I just don't know any more than this place," she said.

"But what about your parents? I mean, I really don't mean to pry, but don't you want answers? Why have you never went looking for them?" I asked.

"Alec, I'm not one for the awkward cliché, but sometimes the answers we need are a lot closer than we think. Besides—for example—when you came to the motel you were in need of answers yourself. I could help you to get to where you needed to go, and I was glad to. As for myself, I have everyone and everything I could need."

I was embarrassed by my interrogation of her personal life. "I'm sorry. Really, I didn't mean to intrude."

She stayed silent. I respected her for her strength. I didn't know who my late brother was, and I freaked out and left my entire family behind. She didn't even know who her own parents were and just accepted that as her fate. The same way the old man said to just accept death, she accepted her lack of family and made better of it than she probably would've had she ventured off to who knows where.

"Your parents, Alec. However much they did or didn't tell you about David doesn't matter; it isn't even your problem to feel. It's not something that you directly have to hold on to forever. I couldn't imagine losing a child. How would I even go about explaining that to my next? All I mean to get at is that in the same way death is irreversible, so are problems that have already happened. You have two choices: Either go on hating your parents for what they didn't tell you and what they failed to realize was important to let you know, or just accept their reasoning. Accept that it was something that maybe they just wanted to hide. Something they wanted to tuck away and bury in mounds of regret and angst only to never look at it again," she explained.

I truly did take her advice. I wanted to speak with my parents. I remembered they were probably worried for me. "Maybe when we get to the shop we can see if they have a phone," I suggested. I would call my parents and apologize for being so irrational, reacting so bluntly and confusedly.

"Most problems are worth dismissing, Alec. If I went around trying to find my parents—that is, if they are still alive—what would they say to me? 'We left you; why did you come find us?' I just made the most of my life, and, to be honest with you, I am happy. I hope they are too," she said.

My problems began to feel miniscule compared to hers. I really did feel bad for my parents. As we pulled into the garage, I felt a relief that I would be able to call my mother. There it was again: the sun was almost completely gone, the sky fading to black. That huge sign I saw last night had once again illuminated the ground in front of it.

We came out of the car, and I saw my truck strapped to the back of a much larger vehicle that had towed it from the motel. The air was once again tense; thick fog swept across the pavement as the night sky approached. The men who worked the shop were all huddled over a fire hurling out of a fifty-five-gallon drum outside the garage doors. I didn't feel as cold as they did; it was like the air didn't affect me as much. It was cold, sure, but more thick than anything. I couldn't get over the feeling that the air was almost saturated, like I couldn't breathe as fast or as efficiently as I wanted to.

I was worried about how much this would cost. I didn't have more than fifty dollars on me at this point since I just up and ran from the diner.

We entered through the side of the shop this time. She led me through a hallway and into the main garage. The smell of engine oil and musty air entered my lungs, something I was more than accustomed to. I felt like I was back in my father's shop. I missed him when I matched this place with his own.

Entering the garage, I was stunned to see how immaculate the condition was. Tools lined the walls so coordinated they were like stripes. The floor had not a single leak or dusty pile of dirt circling around. White walls covered in perfectly hung flags and posters displayed a sight just as pristine as the exterior of the place, which was much more maintained than my father's shop. I chuckled to myself about how much cleaning he would make me do if I told him about my fascination with this place.

"Gabriella, how are you?" a man said, sliding out from under one of the cars he was working on. He was a short man, with buzzed brown hair and a standard blue shop uniform on. There was a softness in his smile, though; at first impression, what she said about him seemed true.

They hugged each other and then stepped back. "So, I have good news and bad news," he said.

"Well, a healthy bit of bad news can always be remedied by some good. Let's hear the damage first," Gabriella replied.

He put his hands to his hips, thinking of how to lay it on us. "Welp. The truck's dead in the water. We tried everything before having to tow it. But listen, son, it seems you did a lot to rig that thing together in the past. You have a good mechanic back home, don't you?" he asked.

"I do most of the work myself. My dad's got a shop back in our town. He tries to teach me, but as you can see, I'm no perfectionist," I joked.

"Well, don't you worry. We'll work this out one way or another. The downside is, it's going to take a few days if we need to work on the engine itself, maybe up to a week. From what Gabriella told me, you're a decent way from home, son," he said.

"Why don't I call my parents? I'm sure they can come pick me up," I said.

"You'd be fortunate to get some service out here, but I'm willing to let you try. Some kid driving drunk struck down a telephone pole just outside the road there, and it knocked us out since last night. Anyway, just through the door there in my office, try the phone and let me know," he said.

I started toward the door and entered his office. Piles of papers lined a messy table stacked a foot high at least. The ground had more dust than the entire rest of the shop. It's as if he just pushed everything to this room and left the rest to be perfect. In the back of the room in his chair, the guy I met the other night sat looking through a book. He was scribbling notes and had headphones on, humming to himself. I tried not to startle him, so I bent and waved toward him. When he saw me, he instantly pulled them off, hurrying to slam the book shut and play off whatever he was doing.

"*What*? What do you want? You're not supposed to be in here, bro," he said in a tone much less inviting than the one I had been accustomed to from our first interaction.

"Your boss is letting me use the phone. I'm just going to see if I can call my mom is all. Weren't you working in the store the other night?" I asked, matching his tone.

"Good luck," he said, disregarding my question entirely. He turned the phone toward me and swung his backpack around over his shoulder. He pushed passed me and right out the door, as if I'd done something to offend him.

I pushed the numbers in the phone, and as it rung I thought of what to say. How could I apologize, tell them I realized what I said wrong or just explain to them what I found? When the ringing stopped, I heard a hello, but it fizzled out.

This was not the usual tension or fuzz disconnecting the phone; it sounded like drowning, like the pitter patter of raindrops filling the line. One drop after another it sounded like the voice was melting away. "*Hello? Hello?*" I started yelling, and the voice on the other end of the phone kept drowning into the line. She started crying. I could barely hear her, but her voice was cracking each word after the next.

I couldn't make sense of it at the time. I was scared, but I didn't know if it was my mother on the line, or if any of that had even happened at all. The line was barely working, so it was easy to justify the signal loss then and there.

I put the phone down. Waiting was worthless. I gave up and started back out toward the shop. Looking toward them, I could tell something was wrong. The guy my age was arguing with the owner. "I'm not doing it. Get that through your thick skull!" he shouted and stormed off.

"Woah, what was that all about?" I asked.

Gabriella looked toward me. "Alec! Good news: We're going to get the truck fixed absolutely free!" she said.

I was confused. I looked to the owner to ask him why, but he looked down in disappointment and started toward his office.

"What now?" I asked.

"Well, we need to convince that guy who just stormed off angrily that it's a good idea to come with us, and then we're all set to go. They even offered to ship the truck out to you when they're finished. All we need to do is bring him some-where back toward your neck of the woods, at least out of this town," she said.

"What, is he trying to get rid of the guy or something?" I asked.

"Not quite… Why don't you go talk to him? He really is a nice man. He's just worried is all," she said.

I started back toward the man's office. Knocking on the door I slowly pushed it open to see the man with his head in his hands.

"Sir, you busy? I can come back. I just—"

"No, no. Come on in. son. Sorry about that. He can be a little rough sometimes is all," he said, lifting his head and motioning to the seat in front of him. "Davey is a little bit of a lost soul. He's been working with me here for as long as he could hold a wrench. He lives here too—got a room upstairs and everything—but this place, this place isn't for him. It isn't for anyone to be stuck here forever. Everyone's gotta go somewhere in life. He's just stuck to the floor—stuck to these people he's trying too hard to impress," he said.

"I don't understand, sir. I apologize, but what does this have to do with me and my truck?" I asked.

"Well, son, I will fix your truck no matter the cost and ship it back to your house free of charge. I learned from a very smart man about helping those who need it the most. The world will have a funny way of paying me back in turn. All I need is for you to convince Davey to leave here and go with you both. He's never left this town not once since I can remember. This place—it has a grip on people. It's too comfortable, too little going on that you can just embrace it and forget about everything else. For Davey, though, that's more than dangerous. He's never been good at managing his free time," he said.

"What do you want me to say to him?" I asked.

"Honestly, son, I'm really sticking my leg out for you and your truck here. Is it too much to ask for you to think of something to say on a whim? Go upstairs and see if you can talk to him. You never know, you two might just hit it off," he said.

It's not like I had any choice. With that I left the office and started toward his room. What the hell was I going to ask him? What he likes most about his town and what he likes least? How could I sell the place I came from?

Other than Aaron, I never really had any close friends. It's funny how growing up you're just around people who are in your school, at your job. It's odd that people go out of their way to "hit it off" with others. The guy was right, though; I had to think of something quick. I guess I just never thought I'd have to.

That's the thing, though: We all just continue up and down our busy streets. Bustling through life we pay no more than little amounts of attention to where we are, other than how to get to school or work and back home. It's rare that we ever stop to smell that oddly familiar scent in our town, see that landmark that's always been a little out of place.

Either way I climbed the steps up into his room. The nerve crept up my back as I half expected him to be crying or sitting at his desk stabbing a knife into the wooden top.

I swung open the door, and without hesitation he barreled past me with two bags in his hands. "Let's just get the hell out of here!" he said.

I was confused. Minutes ago, he was screaming at the owner telling him he would never leave, and now there he was. Maybe I misunderstood; maybe he felt bad. Either way, I accepted that it was easier than I thought and continued down the steps after him.

Chapter 8

Without a second look back, Davey pushed through the garage and out to the car with force. He ripped open the car door with one hand and swung his bag in with the other, then proceeded to slump down into the seat like a child. Looking at us with a cold arrogant stare, he was acting like we were on his time or like he was quickly going to change his mind. I knew I hadn't gotten much of a chance to meet him the previous night, but man, did I wish in that moment I never had to see him again.

Before I really got to know Davey, I would've killed to be anywhere but around him. With a swing of the door, he called out, "If we wait much longer, I'm definitely changing my mind!" and with that Gabriella came running out the front of the shop.

"Let's go, Alec! We got to get some sleep! Big day of driving tomorrow morning."

I turned around to thank the owner, but he was nowhere to be found. As Gabriella began honking, I jogged toward the car and got in.

"Okay, Davey! Don't worry, I got a decent sized room for you! Master suite at the motel, usually ninety-nine dollars a night, yours absolutely free," she said, followed by a sickening smile from him in response.

Free of charge?

"Perfect! Anything beats that shithole I've been sleeping in forever now. It's not even the room that sucks all that much, but the smell. The smell of engine oil and gasoline. I can never escape it. It follows me everywhere. I can smell it on me when I'm out with friends. I can feel it on me even after the longest shower. It'll be nice to get away from that," he said.

Finally, he had decided to say something. An oddly descriptive first set of words, but maybe he wasn't as careless as he looked. I peered at him in the rearview mirror. He at least had some manners for a complete jerk. He sat in the backseat instead of feeling entitled to shotgun. I laughed to myself. Maybe if we were brothers, we would've wrestled over the front seat like Gabriella was our mom taking us to school. Looking down to my hands, I sighed at the thought of my brother once again. I missed him, and I hadn't ever even felt what it was like to be with him.

The road on the way back to the motel was covered in trees that swept over us like waves waiting to crash into the cars below them. I couldn't believe how they swung over the road, engulfing it in their swinging mass. Fun fact about me: I was afraid of the woods as much as I was of the sea. Something about a natural beauty so large and magnificent that you had no idea how to react to it. When you step into the middle of the woods it's like being lost at sea. All around you are foreign objects; no direction, no hope, just a lost and empty feeling in the base of your gut. Navigating that car through the woods was like a boat sailing through the sea. We were on a course, but we had no idea where we were going, and I had no idea who was taking me. The feeling was beautiful but made for all the more a fearful adventure at the very least.

As we arrived back to the motel, I noticed a pub lit up like a city skyline in the middle of the night, a bonfire of lights, and a sea of noises that I hadn't noticed the night before. It was probably closed the first night I arrived in town, and paired with my half-intoxicated angst to find a place for the night, it was no question I had driven right past.

It must have been Davey's regular spot, because as we got out of the car he leaped toward the bar and shouted, "See you guys soon! Thanks for the ride," his arrogant banter paired with a faux smile you could see miles away.

I started back toward the motel trudging to my dungeon, and Gabriella let out a "psst!" motioning for me to follow her up the steps to the second floor. We continued up to a balcony where we sat overlooking the street and the bar across the way. It was beautiful. You could see all the way down the main road on either side for at least a mile. Long away in the distance, further than I had come, there were lights flickering in the night sky. There must've been a city close by, because the buildings were spouting high up into the air, higher than any house, and there were smokestacks with pillows of clouds rolling out of their rooftops.

To the right was the road from which I came; there wasn't a single light for as far as my eye could see. And in front of us, just behind the pub, there were pockets of light raging into the air from the tips of the trees. It was a miracle that town had as dense of forest as it did, because there were at least twenty bonfires raging so high they could be seen from where we were sitting.

Gabriella pulled out two cans, cracked them both, and turned to me handing one over. I read the colorful label, which said, "Cola." Silly me for being excited that she'd hand me a beer.

That night I got to know Gabriella as more than the woman who gave me a ride. That night she told me her memories—memories that seemed to span longer than lives could. She told me of the best guests and even the worst. The governor himself had stopped into the motel once on a traveling tour of businesses.

One guest she told me of she suspected to be a spy. He used to come in an all-black suit and speak very little English, but she said that as soon as she would walk by his room in the night, she could overhear him talking in a fluent tone in sometimes up to seven different languages. When they served him food in the dining room, he would eat very little and request eggs situated at the four corners of his plate, with nothing in the middle.

She went on again laughing and poking fun at all her best times at the motel. Not once did I ask anything too personal out of the care for her happiness that was so vivid and clear as she spoke of the best times of her life. I even started to share a few stories: relationships that fell apart, the first car accident I got into with my parents, what I wanted to do after I got back home.

"You know the chef here? The one you met earlier?" she asked. As she motioned to the roof behind her, there he came. A large stalky man with a gentle and calm face, his shadowy beard blended with his curly black hair. His sleeves were rolled on the white chefs coat he wore, and the beer in his hands complemented his "I had a long day" sigh before taking his first sip.

We exchanged a lot of laughs that night—her, Mariano, and me. He was a very decent man, but after a few too many drinks he had some indecent stories to tell. Either he was working off the alcohol to fuel his imagination or he was one of the most interesting men alive. Hell, if I lived the life he did I'd move to a job in the middle of nowhere myself.

He looked to us with bloodshot eyes and said, "Time for one last story, kids, then I'm off to bed."

When Mariano was young he married his high school sweetheart, and they had three children before he was aged thirty. After twenty years of being a chef by day and a regular father with a mostly normal life, he just decided to get up and leave it all behind. He told us just about everything about himself, except for the part why he left his family.

"All you need to realize is that I had no choice—not a single choice at all," he said.

He went on to tell us that he moved to a country in Europe that he forgot the name of and spent about ten years living under an alias until he met another woman whom he fell in love with. He talked about how beautiful she was and how her personality glimmered in the moonlight like the North Star, like *his* North Star. Long story short, one day she decided to tell him that she was an orphan, or so she had thought, and that she had finally found her long lost family.

Mariano ventured back to America with his new wife to help her meet her new family, and upon arrival had an experience so fateful and mesmerizing I don't think I'll ever actually believe it to be true. The sister of his new wife, the twin of the woman he had fallen in love with, was his first wife that he had left over a decade ago. His ex-wife sat dumbfounded in front of him, and they both locked eyes in disbelief. He had spent years running away from his past, and there it was, all out in front of his eyes for him to deal with.

"And with that, I realized that you can never outrun your decisions. They're always in front of you. You can never make sense of your past. You don't have to make sense of it, though. You know that, right, kids? You don't make sense of it; you just solve it. If it doesn't work, try again. Your past is always going to be there, even after you die. The stuff we carry, that's what weighs on us until the day we can't think no more. I never solved my past, and look at me now. Been stuck here for as long as I can remember," and with that, he got up kicking half of the empty bottles off the balcony and trudged inside to bed.

There was an odd silence in the air—a thick surge of thought that weighed heavy on us for a few minutes. I felt uncomfortable and started to get up and go off to bed when suddenly she grabbed my arm. "A few more minutes, please. I have a story to tell you too," she said.

All of a sudden she asked me about dreams—dreams that I had, ones I couldn't forget. I kept them to myself, but nightmares were all too normal to me. I didn't tell her about the dream I had the night before, or the ones I had in different settings. She told me a dream, though, one I never made sense of until years and years later in my life.

"Alec. Since I was as young as six, I can remember waking up in cold sweats, paralyzed by fear, crying in agony at my loneliness. I hadn't been totally transparent with you earlier. I've been having the same dream, over and over again for years. It happens every single night. It's clearer to me than the days I live.

"In my dream, I'm... I'm floating down a river in a basket. My mother and father are just silhouettes pushing me along. All of a sudden the stream gets widened by a wave, and I get swept up faster and farther than they can catch up to." She began to cry and put her head down, holding her tears back.

I didn't say a word in anticipation of the rest of her story; I didn't want to pry, either. After a long pause, she continued.

"When I finally come down from the wave, they're running so fast, all I can see is the silhouettes with arms stretched wide, tears barreling down from their figures. All of a sudden

I drop, as if from a waterfall or a cliff or something, and they both just turn and walk away from one another. Like they gave up, like they couldn't dive after me. When I fall I feel better. I wake up peacefully. It's not like a nightmare by the end; it's like I'm woken up with the embrace of a hug larger than my body itself."

I tried to make sense of her dream, tried to make meaning and think of a way to respond. "Wow... I mean... I don't know what to say. Have you ever wondered if maybe it has something to do with—"

"I know it has to do with my parents, Alec. But whether I want to find out exactly why they let me fall off that cliff and walked away is a different story," she said, and I in turn kept quiet.

It felt like minutes that we spent up there together, but after hours had passed, we noticed Davey trotting back across the street, hanging on the shoulders of another man. They were obviously drunk, not swaying uncontrollably, but their singing and chanting at the top of their lungs definitely blew their cover.

With that Gabriella chuckled and wished me good luck, continuing off to bed. I followed in hopes that Davey wouldn't see me. So little did I care to hang out with him, and I hoped that so little did he care to do the same with me. Gabriella gave me a different room next to her and Davey's, not the suite but a much larger space at that, and I was happy with it.

As I drifted off to bed that night, I had another strange dream, this one even more disturbing than the last. I was lying down on my back, unable to move, and looking up at the sky. A rectangle cutout appeared above me. It's like I was in a grave, buried alive with no ability to move or speak. Suddenly, my mother popped her head over the hole and looked down at me.

Tears were falling from her eyes and pattering at the opening of the grave, which was covered by some sort of glass. She pounded on it, screaming my name, but it couldn't be broken. I couldn't reply, couldn't even move a single muscle to tell her I was okay. As the dream ended, she finally pounded the glass so hard that it shattered. As the shards fell to my face, I shot up from the bed to see Davey and a stranger had broken into the room. They were standing shoulder to shoulder and said in unison, "Come on, man. Time to get out of this shithole."

"How the hell did you guys get in *here*?" I asked, more intimidated than confused.

"Doesn't matter, man. We're going to have a fire down in the woods. Want to come or not?" the one I hadn't yet met asked.

At the dread of having another night terror, I accepted and followed the two out of the room without thinking. My heart was still pounding on my way down the steps. Catching my breath as I climbed down to the bottom was hard, and I hadn't even realized I was fully awake until I stared at the forest before me: a sea of black that was less inviting than the two had made it sound back up in the room. They yelled for me to follow and skipped into the woods like drunken fools, and I—not being any smarter—decided to follow without any hesitation.

We made our way down to the woods behind the motel and to a spot that had definitely been carved out for this specific purpose. Eddie was the guy who had come along with Davey. He was about the same age as the two of us. His dark curly hair matched his glowing brown eyes. He looked like a happy-go-lucky fun type of guy who cared less and partied more. With his buttoned-down shirt open to the middle and his sandals tripping every other step, I figured I was right by that judgment.

A small firepit between a few logs was the meeting point for endless fires, as they explained it. Eddie told me about people spewing gasoline onto the open flame and fighting over stupid arguments that turned to fist fights. Nothing of what they described appealed to me, and when it got silent, the dark grew thicker and the air much colder.

"Eddie, how long have you lived here?" I said, hoping to inspire any bit of conversation I could.

He smirked, accompanied by a brief chuckle. He replied, "What do you want? A story?"

"I mean, we are out here. Nothing better to do. A story wouldn't hurt to pass the time," I replied.

"Do you know what a story is, Alec? A story's a lie. Not a complete lie, but not complete truth, either. A story is an adaptation. A story has a protagonist; it has some sort of slimy detail accompanying the buildup. You're going to sit there, watching and waiting. Let me ask you something, Alec. If I told you that I got some money from saving up, and I worked hard enough to have money, would you be happy with my story? That's it, just a man working and making some money, and he saves it. Nothing and no one else involved in the story, no one there to ruin anything or make it harder on the man. Just the simple act of completing a goal."

I couldn't tell if he was testing me. That was such a long-winded response to such a subtle question. The happy and fun-loving guy I judged was quickly swapped with a jerk no more welcoming than Davey. I wasn't intimidated—just more puzzled. Who was this guy to ask me questions like a teacher? Still, with the two of them, I was vulnerable, so I played into his game. "No, I wouldn't be happy. Nothing happened in that story. I mean, something happened, but not really," I replied.

"Exactly, Alec. Something happened, actually. I wanted money and got it. Something happened for me, but not for you. See, in my story, nothing bad happened. Nothing that could make you think you're better than me or the people in it. That you're glad it didn't happen to you. That you're glad you played your cards right and that you can just go back home and act like the story was all fiction. Know what, Alec? Boy, do I have a story for you," he started. His drunken tone was harder to follow than his confusing attitude, but out of lack of choice I decided to keep quiet.

"Eddie, take a break on the drinks, and calm the fuck down. Give the kid a break," Davey started.

"Don't worry, brother. I'm not doing anything. I won't even startle the little guy," he said, darting a perplexing gaze into my eyes.

The fire felt hotter than before. The air fell silent around us. The moon tucked behind the clouds hid all the moonlight we once had. It seemed almost like his story controlled the setting, but of course it was just coincidence. His gaze stayed locked on me. I could barely see anything but his eyes and the outline of his face reflecting off the fire.

"My story starts at home. There's a boy…" he started, taking another sip of his drink. The moonlight shone again through the clouds, and light persisted. I could see Davey again. For some reason that made me feel safer.

"The boy has no parents. None that matter, that is. His dad is gone. On a work trip that's lasted over three years now. He's twelve years old, an only child, and his mom couldn't care if he's dead or alive. Do you see him yet, Alec? Do you feel him yet? Because every night he sat up and cried about his situation. Every night he sat up and cried when he heard random men slip in and out of his house, patting his head and slapping his mom on their way in and out. There was a man who this boy knew. Who he trusted. You ready? Here comes the light at the end of the tunnel.

"See, there's this man, and he takes a liking to the boy. He teaches him things his absent father never did. How to tie a tie for an interview. How to drive a car. How to make breakfast for his mother in the morning, only to see it tossed to the side for a needle and some lowlife companion. Then all of a sudden, one day the man says he wants to meet the boy's parents. He wants to introduce himself and learn more about the situation—see if he can help. He comes over, he helps the boy set the table, overlooks all the shit the boy is in. Overlooks his makeshift bed under the kitchen table, overlooks the garbage all over the place, just sees him. Just sees someone who needs helping. And when the mother finally comes out of her room with her lowlife companion, what do they do? They shun him away. Yell in his face about what the fuck he's doing in *their home*! And right there. Right fucking there, man, do you know what they lied about?"

I could see the tears in his eyes building. Suddenly his intimidating gaze was exchanged for a soft and sorrowful welling of tears fighting to race down his cheeks. I had a feeling this story wasn't a lie. That this story was quite the opposite. I cooperated and replied in sync as best I could, "What was that, Eddie?" I returned in a fragile tone trying not to show my fear.

"That that shithole—that dump where all those men had come in and out, and where all my tears had flooded over and over until I *drowned* in them—that that house was anything near a home! That was the biggest story I have ever been told," he replied.

I could see Davey out of my peripheral, looking into the blackness. It looked so deep, much deeper than your average forest. It was like we'd been transported to the bottom of the ocean, and we were awaiting something—something that could come from all sides of us. I felt it behind me, and then in front of me. But him, he was just staring at it. Staring like it helped him make sense of something instead of fear. Before I could ask him, Eddie continued.

"So, you know what happened to the man—to the one person in the boy's entire life who ever showed him a hint of belonging? He got a punch to the jaw from the lowlife boyfriend, and when he finally got to his feet, he fled. Without a word he fled faster than the boy's father the day he left, faster than his teachers the day his mother ripped him out of school. With him, any light surrounding the boy had fled too. It was dark all around him. His eyes focused on that man—the lowlife boyfriend. The man screamed at the boy, shook him, and rattled him about bringing strange men into the house. But *he* was a strange man; he needed to be gone. In the boy's blind rage, he took a knife from the kitchen counter, and he made the lowlife go away. He made him disappear as fast as the man had run out the door. That's all he did. He didn't mean to hurt him, he just needed him to go away. He wanted him to leave them alone once and for all. And the boy felt much pain in the days to come. So much pain that he gave up, so much pain that the life before him crumbled, until he wound up in front of this fire. Telling stories that could be lies. Telling ones that he wished were lies, but they were as true as it comes. The boy wished he could tell lies and then go home and act like it was all fiction."

I felt a panging—not in my chest, but in my whole body. I was overwhelmed with emotion. I couldn't believe what he just said. He killed someone. I didn't know what shock felt like, but I assume that's what I was experiencing. I looked over to Davey; he was staring at me with a full smirk, waiting for my first reaction. I had nothing. I wasn't mad; I just felt confused. I felt bad for Eddie. In some way, he was justified in being angry. Neglect was the only form of love he ever knew. Killing someone, though—in cold blood—that made my insides turn to a sludge that struggled to move fast enough to let my body turn.

"Here, with Davey and the rest of the family, we all get each other. We all understand what we've been through and accept it. We can't be fixed, but we can achieve happiness. That's what He tells us," he started.

"Eddie. Quit it now or else he's gonna run back up to that friend of his and never look at us again. You're shit-spitting again, and it's not making us look any less crazy than we already come off," Davey said.

"Man, am I glad we're out here, bro." He sat back, taking another sip.

I sat back, taking another sip. "So, man, this group you're a part of—"

"We're a family, and we're the most powerful around. Don't think twice about calling it a *group* around the wrong people. Especially not around me," Davey said, not looking me in the eyes. He just peered at me through his peripheral. Even he didn't believe what he was saying.

I could hear the lack of integrity in his voice. I caught on to the lies he so easily passed out as the truth. This Davey was much more lost and alone than he made himself feel, like he was constantly reassuring himself of his power and companionship that was never there.

"So, then, the family. Where are they? I mean, if you were so close to them, why haven't they come to find us, or you? Why haven't they called?"

"It's not about calling, man. It's not about finding. They'll find me, don't worry. Even if I do go east or wherever it is you guys are taking me. They'll give me my way back."

Now he was starting to freak me out. Who the hell is this kid involved with? Some sort of gang family, maybe; it has to be something someone's heard of on the news or something. But he himself—no way was he as bad as he came off.

"Now listen, man," he said, crunching his beer against his knee. After letting out a painfully unwelcome belch he continued, "I don't need to talk to you about this, about anything. You know nothing about what I've gone through, about what I've had to do—not a single thing. So just leave me alone and drink your beer. Sooner we finish this the sooner I can stop listening to you and whoever else you came with."

"Hey, man, I'm just here trying to catch a glimpse at a shooting star," I replied, acting uninterested. "If you want to tell a story like Eddie did, I'm all ears. I am a good listener. And he told a good story at that," I said, trying to discredit the truth of what Eddie said, as if to bring any normality back to the conversation that I could.

"There are no good stories," he said. "Just a bunch of people exaggerating memories that they think mean more to others than themselves. It's a lie we tell ourselves to think anything we do matters. All I've done in the past few years is lie, kill, steal, and drink. It's probably all I'll ever do, but I'm not sad. Couldn't give a fuck for anything otherwise, anyway."

"I gotchu, man," I replied, trying not to stir any unwanted anger from the two of them. I had come to realize I probably shouldn't have followed them out that door, and I couldn't tell if it was too late to go back. I decided to play it cool, act unfazed.

"Well, man, sounds like you've been through hell and back."

"Trust me, kid, I've been to hell; still living in it. It's the getting back part I'm trying to figure out." And with that he pulled open another beer and turned away, staring back into the blackness.

Chapter 9

———

For quite some time we just sat around the fire, huddled together in the blackness. I had to have drunk another three or four beers before someone finally said something. All that time Eddie and Davey were just sitting there, staring at nothing. The silence was as thick as the blackness that entranced them. They were comfortable with it, but for me the silence only created more noise—a white noise that was louder than the crackling of the firewood. The air was sharp and cold enough to mask the smell of smoke; instead, the smell was just blank. It was as blank as the night they stared into, but it must've brought them some kind of comfort.

Each minute of it felt like an hour, adding weight to my shoulders. The heat on my back was overwhelming, even though the flames were in front of me. I didn't feel safe there with them. I just wanted the night to be over with so I could head back and be done with those people. And then he finally spoke.

"All right, Eddie, I've had enough of this, and I got a plan. I think it's time we take young Alec here on that extra special adventure we've got planned. How 'bout you?" Davey started.

"I couldn't agree more, brother. And are we thinking of the same host for our mighty fine evening to come?" Eddie returned.

That was the time, the perfect time for me to tell them, the last chance I had to never be a part of what it is they wanted to do. That's the thing about life, though: every single choice is a paradox of what could've led into the next decision. I could've decided never go to with them, but I could've also decided never to leave the hotel room or accept Gabriella's ride. Hell, my parents could've never decided to have me. I didn't want to be there anymore, though. I just wanted to go back to the motel and sleep. "Uh, hey, guys, I think I should head back. We don't have time for an adventure. It's, like, three in the morning already. Plus, that girl back there, she's my only ride."

Davey chuckled, followed by, "Don't worry, little man. There's much more time than you think. Plus, Eddie here has a ride of his own. We can come back here any time you like. We just want you to see what it's like to become a real man. Isn't that right, Eddie?"

"Come on, man. I just told you a story about how I killed some guy, and you made me do it. You got me all depressed. Now let's just do something to make us feel a little more upbeat, a little more fulfilled in who we really are," Eddie said.

I was trapped at a crossroads. The alcohol in my system more than lagged my decision making, and the fear of saying no to the two of them only furthered my opposition to my idea of heading back. At the same time, however, I felt a lot safer with Gabriella at the motel. She never spewed any nonsense about killing people or being part of some family of rejects. At fault of my kindness, I brushed off my gut feelings and continued onward. "All right, guys, let's see what this old town has to offer. Anyway, it couldn't be much, seeing as what I got to see in the daylight."

"Oh, now that's where you're wrong, little guy. Night is where all the fun comes out to play," Davey said.

Before I could ask how we were going to extinguish it, Eddie had unzipped his pants and was putting out the fire his own way. "What? I'm not going to waste any good beer, am I?"

They acted like fools; like animals. They were both so misguided. I mean, I can't say I am the perfect outfit of what a human should be, but really? Pissing out a fire and talking about being beasts of the night in some shanty town hours outside of the city. Davey bragging about being a killer and thief. All the while when I studied them, all those minutes when they were staring off into the blackness, I noticed something.

There was a calmness to them. There was a calmness to *both* of them. I was afraid of what they said and what was coming next, but when they sat there staring, I wasn't afraid of them. The darkness is what got me. Eddie was right about his stories: It made me grateful I had been raised by loving parents even if I didn't have it all. I felt bad for him more than I despised him. I didn't know about Davey, though. He kept staring at me like I shouldn't trust him. Like he wanted me to despise him for some reason.

When the fire was totally out all that shone through the trees was the light of the moon, which was intermittently fading between the clouds. I always hated the forest. The woods were home to creatures and animals, and at night all their features were more than accelerated. I could feel this urge all around me. Darkness was gripping me like a constrictive hug, tighter and tighter until we finally reached the road's edge. I felt the comfort of a streetlamp a few dozen yards to my left. That little glimpse of light made all the difference when I was standing there in the dark.

"Come on! Get in!" took me away from that light faster than I had hoped for, and I turned away to the dark street to see the red taillights of Eddie's car. I approached it; its black frame looked pristine in the moonlight. Unlike my truck, this car actually was nice. Black leather seats complemented by red stitching were much nicer than the cheap "Fresh Car" scent dangling in the rearview mirror. I was actually jealous of Eddie's ride.

"How did you get a car like this, man? I mean, what do you do for work?" I said over the rumbling of screaming voices on the radio. He turned it down. "Don't worry about what I do for work. The family takes care of us all, man! You'll see if you want to!"

Again with that weird family. If I heard about this family one more time, I'd ask them to bring me to their house that instant.

"So, what do you have east there that we don't, city boy? Anything us creatures might like to explore? I mean, you are taking me to the city, right? Once I get out of this place?" Davey started.

"No, I don't live in the city, actually. About an hour out. My house is in a town not much different than this one. I actually came out here because my family has a cabin here."

"Yeah, I know. That old brown lodge with the bright red door right off the main road," Davey replied.

"Yeah. How'd you know that?" I replied.

"Oh, a mystery. How do I know? Well, my uncle has lived here way longer than me, of course. He knows everyone around here. All the property owners and families that've been here for generations."

"Hey, brother. We're here, man," Eddie said.

I looked over to my right. Suddenly we were in a zone much less rural than before, with rows of houses like an average suburb. The air was still crisp enough to block base layer scents, but I could catch smoke in the distance from ongoing chimney fires. One house a few away from us had no lights turned on. That is what Eddie was pointing to. I won't lie, for a few guys who said we were going to be having a ball of a night, this didn't seem like much fun.

"What? Is there some kind of surprise party for me in there?" I asked jokingly.

"Yeah, think of it that way. If we bring back what he wants, I'm sure you'll have some sort of party, even if it isn't a surprise one," Eddie said.

"Let's go pay our friend here a little visit, shall we? One last time," Davey started.

His tone was much too sinister for me to believe there were any real friends in that house, but how bad could it be? These guys barely knew me. Why would they do anything wrong in front of me? I could just report them to the local authorities. Unless they killed me and dumped my body. I shut myself up; they wanted to have fun. I'm sure it was a mindless endeavor. We came down from the car. Every second of warmth I spent in the car reminded me how cold the wind outside was.

When we approached the house, I noticed a significant difference in the attention this owner paid to their property. The grass had to have been over a foot tall, and it just cut off at the next lawn that was perfectly trimmed no later than a few days before. The paint on the house was chipped, and mildew grew on the places that were still colored. The consistency of the suburban style houses was disrupted by this odd and almost decrepit neighbor.

Davey ran around the side and waved us on to follow. "What the hell are we doing?" I asked.

"What do you think, dummy? He's our friend; he's not expecting us. We're gonna try and scare him," Eddie said.

After trying three others, Davey found a window that would open. He took a small blade out from his side pocket and traced it along the edge of the screen. Now I was skeptical. Who breaks into their friend's house with a boxcutter just to surprise them? My doubt was outweighed by the cold, and

I continued in after them. I'm not terribly overweight, but the few pounds I could've shed instead of gaining in the last few months might've helped me with my window slipping operations. My fall was anything short of graceful, and as I plummeted in, Davey and Eddie both put their pointer fingers to their lips and pointed for me to stay under the table.

Davey pointed toward the basement door and then his watch and put up three fingers. I'm guessing he meant for me to wait until they came back. I could hear music in the distance. It wasn't from a stereo, though. When it cut out, I could hear the warp of a needle coming off a record player. How dumb could I have been? How stupid could I have been to think we were actually in their friend's house?

All the lights were off, and I could only see pictures on the wall in old black and white where the moon shone through the windows. Not pictures of family on tropical vacation or something. There were photos of soldiers toting guns and standing tall at the base of a jungle. Another showed five men lined up outside of a helicopter, one who stood on crutches with one leg bandaged up. The kitchen hadn't been updated in years, and there wasn't any television in the living room. Either these guys have really old friends, or I just fell for something really bad.

I started to move out from under the table so I could leap out the window. Screw these guys. I don't even know why I cared to be around them in the first place. Now they had me here doing who knows what in some old couple's house. Before I could make my first move, I heard a footstep coming down the stairs. As he walked, I slowly crept out and stood up as quietly as I could. It was too late; I could hear him walking up behind me. Before I could make any noise, he brushed past me, just missing my shoulder, and closed the window before me. I stood silent as a mouse. The lights were still off. The only thing I could hear was the pounding of my own chest.

"I can feel you," he said.

He turned toward me. I sat in shock. What had I just done? I broke into some old man's house out of the judgment of these two delinquents, and I was going to be the one to get caught for sitting under a dining room table. His head was locked on me, then his gaze faded. He started looking to the left and then right. He put his hands out in front of him, but they were still a few feet from me. I shuddered and then held my breath for as long as I possibly could. When his eyes finally shone in the moonlight, I realized. I realized why his record player was on, but he was the only person on the street with no lights on in his house—why he hadn't sensed me after I sat in silence, frozen in time.

A bang sounded in the basement, and he instantly shifted himself toward the door. When he did, I darted toward the window and pulled it up. He started down the stairs with his hands brushing the walls on either side of him. I was in too much disbelief to even register where I was. I scraped my wrists on the way out. I couldn't feel the pain, but I saw the blood and kept running. I ran until I was back at the car a few houses down. The idea of running off went through my mind but was quickly subdued by the idea of freezing to death, not knowing where the hell I'd be going. What if I just told the neighbors what had happened? Maybe they would help me. Before I could decide to evade the car and try to run as far as I could, out the front door came Davey and Eddie. The two beeps of the car unlocking went off by my side, and I instantly yanked open the door and got inside.

"Holy shit, that was close!" Eddie said, slamming the door beside him. "Where the fuck were you, kid?" he asked, looking at me through the rearview mirror.

"What just happened?" I asked, drowned in my seat, eyes wide staring in the mirror.

"We just robbed that man blind! Huh! Get it? 'Cause the guy's blind!"

"Shut up, Eddie. That doesn't make anything we did any more honorable. We're just doing it on orders of the family, nothing else," Davey said, looking back at me.

"I want to go back to the motel. I demand you take me back to the motel, then do whatever the hell it is you guys wanna do for the rest of your night. This isn't my idea of a good time. We just committed a crime!" I said, this time in outrage.

"Will you just calm yourself? So what, we lifted some gold and an old trinket off an army vet. Nothing I haven't done before. He's not any better than us anyway, you should know," Davey started in defense. "That guy's a bad man. He's killed more than all of us combined. Went off to war and killed, came back crazy and killed some more. Lost his eyes pouring bleach into them after going crazy and saying he didn't wanna see what he did anymore. Now, does that sound like someone who you should feel bad for robbing, Alec?"

"Doesn't matter what kind of person he was. You don't rob someone based on who they are. You don't rob someone because no one deserves to get their stuff stolen! It's a crime," I said.

Davey stared at me in the rearview mirror. His gaze softened but his tone stayed tough. "Well, this is what the family needs—to get stronger. Now just leave it alone and we'll all be on our merry way come tomorrow, *all right*?" Davey demanded. "We can't bring you back now. It's too late. You're gonna tell that woman, and she's probably gonna tell my uncle, and then I'll never get out of this place. This is the only way. Eddie did what he had to do, solidified his fate, and now he's good to stay. I just wanted to help him before bailing one last time."

I was overtaken again. Emotion flooded through me like a plane window burst in midair. It started raining heavily—so heavily that I couldn't hear their voices. Davey was talking to Eddie, Eddie's head swirling in excitement as he turned up the radio, but all I could hear was rain. Rain was drowning out everything until it suddenly stopped. It cleared, and Davey turned to me.

"I'm sorry, all right? We should've warned you. Being bad is our thing. It's just how it is. It's how we make it right."

I knew then why his uncle so badly wanted him to leave. Why he so badly wanted him to get out of this place. Now that we committed a crime, what if they came searching for us? I'm sure someone would. I am too young to be doing this. Who was I kidding? I've done my fair share of regretful living before coming here. That doesn't justify it; I couldn't even try to justify what we just did. I sat in silence and disbelief.

"Don't worry. We just have to take this to the family. I'm sure it will square our debts, then it's off with you come sun's up tomorrow. All right, man?"

"Yeah, man, he's right. Being bad's all we know. But we're trying to make it right. This is how it starts, okay? Really, I'm sorry too. We should've warned you," Eddie said.

Whatever consolation that brief apology could've given, I accepted.

As we drove off from the house, I could see the old man standing by his door. I felt so sorry for him. There he was, staring up into the moonlight that he could only just feel but not truly see. I wonder if he remembered what it was like to see. What it was like to appreciate colors. What it was like to look in the mirror at himself. Who would bleach their own eyes? Maybe Davey was right: If he did kill real people, maybe he did feel like a monster. Like my grandfather said, though, who knows what he had kept inside him.

I wasn't wrong. In a weird way I also felt for Eddie and Davey. Davey stared at the man all the way down the street as much as he could until he caught me with his head cocked back, staring at his regret, and he straightened out his head to hide his shame. I think what I said really got to him. He clapped hands with Eddie and they sang in unison, but I could see in both of their eyes and their hands what they didn't want to admit—regret. I could see from their fragmented movements, the way they kept slowly and longingly sliding their palms over their entire faces. They felt something. They really felt more than pissing on a fire and stealing from a blind man and then running off like it was nothing to them.

I know how they felt because they matched my body movements the first time I felt regret.

It was the late afternoon, I remember that. It was hot, the sun was beaming on me. That's why I left; I remember that. The exact day, the time, the road I don't remember. The feelings, though, from the sun to the decision to the regret, I remember those—all of them.

"Hey, Aaron! I gotta go, man. I gotta go!" I screamed over the sound of the music. I had a midterm exam to study for. I promised myself I wouldn't go that day, but there I was. Cold beer, an open field, and women outnumbering men—it was more than a perfect substitute for a morning spent studying.

I said my goodbyes and headed for my truck. At fault of the alcohol, I struggled to get up into my seat, laughing at myself when I finally entered. Okay! Let's go, big guy! I said to myself, slapping my cheeks with open palms before shifting into drive. I curved out of the field and headed back toward the road, feeling the cool breeze filling my sleeve and lifting the cloth on my shoulder. I embraced the wind and turned the music high enough to drown out the exhaust leak I'd been ignoring for months.

When I peeled out of the driveway, I started toward my house. I wasn't nearly halfway there when it happened. He just leapt out in front of me, just appeared there out of nowhere. I was afraid, and my heart fell to the bottom of my stomach. I pumped the brakes and again felt the regret of another fix needed when it wasn't enough to stop me in my tracks. I hit him. I hit him, and without a doubt I killed him. I swung the door open and fell out of the driver's side door.

I came around the front of the truck and saw the blood and fur on the front of my bumper. I didn't know what to do. It was an accident; I didn't mean it. I didn't do it on purpose. I looked under the truck; there he was, lying motionless. I knew exactly who it was. Betsy's dog, Scoot, was the main attraction at all her birthday parties, all the school events he attended, and I just killed him. I pulled him by his legs—a mix of drunkenness and panic caused me to drag him out from under the truck. I could see her house in the distance. No one was outside, which meant that they hadn't come looking yet.

The blood was warm on my hands. I panicked, grabbing a cloth from my truck bed and cleaning my hands as fast as possible. I pulled him down beside the road, wiped my hands again on the already blood-soaked cloth, and leapt back into the truck. I drove to the nearest full-service car wash. I must have paid for three or four cycles so I could wash all the blood and fur off and run it into the drain below.

Later that week when we were all in school, Betsy was sitting behind us at a table panting and screaming about her dog. Her mom had just found him at the roadside where I left him. My friends looked around swearing and raving about

"what asshole would hit someone's dog and just leave it there?"
My hands started to sweat; I rubbed my open palm languidly
down my face again and again as my movements became
fragmented. I craned my neck back to Betsy until she caught
me but not my regret, and just as Davey had, I turned away
before she could notice.

Chapter 10

___

"All right, gents, on to the teacher we go," Eddie started, cutting the music off.

"The teacher?" I asked. "Who's the teacher?"

"Well, only the one guy who has us out in the middle of the damn night doing what we have to do, that's who," Eddie replied.

We continued on down a dark and dusty path in the woods. I remember smelling fire from at least a mile away. When I was back in my hometown that smell brought a sense of calm. Someone was huddled by a fire, roasting marshmallows, talking about old times with their best friends. In that place, fire meant something far more sinister. It felt like the air around me was closing in as we got closer to it. There was this grasp that the smoke had. It filled the air with remorse and guilt instead of nostalgia and excitement.

"Stop here, Eddie. We can go along on foot," Davey said.

I'd be lying if I said I wasn't scared half out of my mind at that point. The night was as dark as the color black itself. The trees were so thickly settled that moonlight ceased to exist beyond that point. I felt twinges of fear tickling the sides of my forehead, shaking the tips of my fingers. We could see it from the edge of the road. Like a North Star, the fire was so large and thick it could be seen from a hundred yards away. It was the only thing that illuminated the woods before us. I tiptoed through the forest, taking cautious and slow steps to make sure I wouldn't fall or twist my ankle.

When we finally came to a clearing where the base of the fire was, I couldn't believe my eyes. Dozens of young men and women lined up in military fashion. Their hands were glued to their sides, their eyes darting up to the man at the head of the crowd. And there he was.

There he was, front and center like a politician on a campaign rally or a dictator in front of his subjects. There was an instant tone in the air that let off sinister vibes, but I couldn't quite place them. There I was, an hour from my house where I hadn't expected anything like that to be taking place, and these people were lined up like an army of who knows what peering ahead at this man. And then he started, the words that I remember to this exact day.

"The trees don't blow in the wind, they twist in it. The sky doesn't sit in the air, it falls from it. And the sun, the sun doesn't hide in the clouds, they swallow it—swallow it until your neural transmission believes you are no longer happy. Who let happiness reign in the sun? Who hid bad in the dark? Who suppressed the chaos of life, and buried in fear, your memories of death? Who taught you that good is always in the light, aware to the naked eye? For if ignorance is bliss, how could seeing the light bring such a feeling?"

I turned to Davey and Eddie. They had both fallen into line ahead of me, hands buried in their hips, eyes peeled on the man who stood before them. He was powerful, his stance was both soft yet durable. His voice was smooth as silk, each word as mesmerizing as what came before it. It was as if he was talking to me directly. He stood at the head of dozens of people, but I felt his words as if they were whispers into my own ears.

In his closing statements he said, "Fine young men and women. We have another night, and tomorrow a new day. With that, be who you are. For I will not judge you. I will embrace whatever person you may turn out to be. Each day that comes after the next, I will love you time and again, even if no one else will." And with that he turned and got off the podium from which he stood. The crowd dispersed silently; small whispers made their way around as people fled to each corner of the woods. I could then see smaller fires lit up at different areas around the forest, like each person had their place.

They weren't all wearing the same clothes or had hair grown out to the edge of their backs, but they seemed like a cult. Their congruence in tone and prose was fascinating. It's like the steps they took were all the same size, the way their hands waved was not an inch off from the person beside them; they were all so content. For some reason, though, I was intrigued, and when Davey told me we were to meet the man at the head of the crowd, I was fascinated.

As we got closer to approaching the man, he turned slowly as if our footsteps were anticipated. A large brooding smile swept across his face. He was a clean cut, regular looking gentleman. He seemed as if he showered regularly, teeth straighter than mine, and not a person who lived remotely in the woods full time.

"Ah! Eddie and Davey, my two favorite sons. I anticipate good news from your latest quest, my sweet, sweet children!" he said, holding his hands out. Davey grabbed the artifact from his pocket. It was hard to see from the dullness of the light and his swift movement. "There it is. The machine that man used to put dozens in harm's way, killing who knows how many others. It's important for us to keep these things to ourselves, boys. You did good today." And with that, he turned and gave the pistol to another boy behind him who placed it in a small trunk and walked off.

He then turned to me. "And you, sir. You must be Alec," he said. How he knew my name I hadn't a clue, but before I could ask he kept going, "You didn't think poorly of my words earlier, did you? I get so nervous when I speak to all my children," he said.

His children? I had no idea why he was referring to all these people as his kids. I instantly knew there was something more to it, but I was in such a compromising position that I almost had to just go with it.

"That's the last time. Right, sir?" Davey asked.

The man looked down, smiling at his feet, and said, "Oh, Davey, you can't escape who you are. You're too good at being you. If we aren't ourselves in this world, who are we left to be?"

"You said this would be it. We almost got stabbed by some crazy old dude; he chased us out of the house! What else do you want? For one of us to end up dead again?" Eddie asked.

"Gentleman, you have only but touched the surface for young Alec here. He's not even tried to unlock his potential. He doesn't even know what we have to offer him," he said, peering at me as he turned slowly in my direction. "Boys, listen. When I was your age, I thought I wanted the same thing. I thought that being a good member of society and working toward a fabricated goal that *they* told me was worth it would be all I needed."

Another boy brought a chair to put behind him, and with that he sat. He pulled a knife from his pocket and began to peel an apple handed to him by one of the other people around.

"I used to crave happiness so much so that it consumed me. Happiness was success in the eyes of my peers. It was attained alongside money, class, maybe even love if you're lucky. But one day I made one mistake. One single step out of line cost me all of that. I was banished by my peers, and I lost everything in the process. So, you know what I did?" he said, taking his first bite, somehow his eyes locked on all three of us at the same time. "I just accepted who I was. I just accepted my own version of happiness. Happiness is a state of mind, boys. I'm happier today then I was when I was chasing it. In my own version, whether everyone agrees with it or not, this is my state of success, and all I want to do is teach you all that you don't need to try so damn hard all the time. Just be kids, and then young adults, and then let it come to you in its own way," he said.

His gaze was instantly more malicious than his presence gave off. I thought to ask different questions. Why did their people stand like an army of peers? What did his speech mean? Where were we exactly? All I could feel was the heat of the fire pressing against my back. I turned to it to give my back a break and waited to let Davey and Eddie respond to the man.

After a few moments the silence was broken, not by them but by me. "The fire? Why such a huge fire out in the middle of nowhere?" I asked.

"True power," the man replied almost instantly. He walked past me as I stood in awe of the flames almost thirty feet off the ground, "Alec, flames swallow whatever they engulf whole. Flames aren't a warning that danger is coming, they're danger embodied in its true self," he said with his arms spread out toward the fire.

"Yes, but I don't understand what you said. It was a creative speech, but the world doesn't swallow itself, and the sky isn't constantly falling toward us. It's keeping us in right where we are," I replied.

He turned to me ever so slightly and put his finger right up before my face and replied, "Alec, the sky is just a culmination of eyes. Each star is a bystander to the life you live. Who knows, cameras could be shuttering so fast you don't see them blink. During the day when the sun hides them, the stars could be taping your every move, seeing each thing you do. So, we start this fire—this tiny star of light right down here on the ground. It points right back up at them. It's a rebellion, a promise that we can be just as noticeable, just as bright right down here on the surface, and we aren't afraid to be seen! The only thing we're afraid of is to be seen as anything that we aren't, so we embrace who we were meant to be!"

Eddie and Davey both looked down in obedience, not excited by the man's tone but also compliant, nonetheless. I tried to stare at them until one of them noticed me, but the man interjected before either of them could. "Alec. You seem to not like anything I have said here today. Why don't you give me another chance? Tomorrow you'll spend the day with Eddie and Davey. See what we do here. The life we offer to those who just want to be who they are without judgment. Spend a night here with us. See what we have to offer, my son," he said.

"Sorry, but I actually have my own place to stay tonight. Speaking of which, I should probably get back to that now. What do you guys think?" I asked.

"We're already here, Alec. It's the middle of the night. Let's just relax. You can meet the others as well!" Davey replied.

I was petrified. Stone cold sober, the fear had knocked every last drop of alcohol from my system. Peering at the fire before me; the slender smile of the man. Once he had turned to the fire and been fully shone in the light, his true flaws started to show. He slipped a cloak off his back, and with that shone his belly, small and round, tucked under his shirt. His ears were pointed and frail, nails long and unattended to. I couldn't see his face, but the hair on his head was thin and grey. He had made almost an entire transformation in the seconds since he took off his covering.

I wasn't welcome here, not in the way they made it seem. I was growing angry as well as fearful of what was to come, but I had no choice, nowhere to run.

With the idea that there were members spread out all over those woods, I was basically surrounded, so I agreed and followed the two to their bunks. Davey and Eddie had set me up in their cabin, which was quaint but quite nice given the situation.

We didn't say much else to each other for the remainder of the night, and I laid wondering what this place may be. I didn't know what I had gotten myself into at that point, and once everything was settled, I remembered the man we had stolen from just hours ago. I remembered his face as he felt the defeat of our escape when we drove off. I began to cry ever so slightly under my breath. How had I come to being involved in such a dreary situation? How did this have anything to do with my relationship with my brother and what I wanted to know about him?

I did what I normally do when I am afraid. I prayed that God would protect myself and my friends and family and watch over the cabin I slept in. The weirdest part, however, was that for the first time I felt like the prayers weren't heard. My usual imaginable forcefield wasn't felt. The normal sweeping hope that settled in me was not around. Instead, I continued to breath that thick and dreary air. The smell of fire smoke burned all throughout the night.

I slept that night and had yet another night terror. This one felt more real than the last. I got up from the screaming of my name being yelled across the forest. I pulled open the door of the cabin to find no fire, no smell of smoke. All I heard was the pattering of rain; all I felt was the beads of water showering down from the sky and laying claim to my unclothed skin. My voice rang through the forest like a bell from the highest tower. Suddenly, I saw my mother and Gabriella running toward me screaming my name. They came up to me, and my mother hugged me with the tightest embrace I had ever felt. She said my name over and over until I asked her what was wrong. She kept hugging me, kept screaming my name, but she couldn't hear me. I was right there, being held by her, but she didn't hear a single word. I looked up to see Gabriella peering at me as she said, "Come back to me, Alec. Come back to the motel, please," and with that I burst up out of my slumber to see Davey and Eddie getting dressed.

"Let's go, man. We'll get you back to the motel all right," Davey said.

"But Davey, we promised your boss that we were going to take you away from here. I thought you slept at his shop. What even is this place? How do you even know that man from last night?" I asked one question after the other.

"It's better that you know less than you want to. Let's just get you back and you can tell my uncle I ran off to some nuclear family and had the time of my life. The teacher is right: This is my home. It has been for some time now. Let's go," he said in a sterner tone than the last.

As we started back toward the car, I was stunned to see that all the fires that raged all throughout the night were still going. Someone must have been walking around all night making sure they didn't die out. The symbolism behind them fascinated me. I genuinely wanted to learn more about what these people did, who they were. I feared the more I tried to learn, though, the deeper I would get trapped in those woods.

The further we walked it felt like the more eyes peered at us. I didn't understand why but people were looking at us from almost all angles. The more we walked back toward the entrance of this place where we came, the more eyes closed in on us, until Davey and Eddie looked to me and said, "Run and don't look back."

At that moment I knew we were somewhere we couldn't easily turn back from. I wished more than anything to be back at my home, sitting on the balcony, pondering what I would do for the day with the morning dew collected on the grass. Instead, the dew peeled through my sneakers as I moved so swiftly that it piled until it bled through my shoes.

I trusted Davey and Eddie to know just where it was we were going, and I ran at an even pace with them as everyone huddled behind us in unison. I took one look around as I felt the impending force of a thousand eyes staring us down from behind. There they all were, hands by their sides, peering at us as if we were the person at the head of the group, the center of attention.

When we got to the edge of the forest, at the foot of the road the car was nowhere to be found. I first just thought we had come out at a different spot in the woods, but we ran up the road about one hundred yards before Davey and Eddie began to lose their focus. "Fuck, you have got to be kidding me!" Davey said.

"Do you think he knew? How the fuck could he have known?" Eddie said, peering back at Davey.

Their angst grew on me, and I fell just short of panic without knowing what they had gotten us caught up in. Before I could get a single word out to ask them what was wrong, two men jumped out of the woods and struck them both in the back of the head with clubs. Not a second after another strike hit me from behind, followed by a slight tingle down my spine, and then nothing but blackness swallowed me whole.

Chapter 11

———

The next part of my life is where things start to get hazy. The world started twisting in mystical ways, and my life flashed before my eyes more than once. In many moments I thought that if I had just stayed in the motel room and not followed Davey to that fire, I would've never learned what I needed to know.

My eyes felt heavy, like they were fighting to put me back to sleep. I felt a panging in the back of my head. It started at the base of my neck and spread like wildfire all throughout my skull. I could feel blood dripping from my nose, and my face was so close to the ground I could've tasted it had I stuck out my tongue.

The more I woke the more I heard the groans of other people around me. When I finally came to, I squirmed to pull my arms out to get up when suddenly I felt them tied together. I was on my stomach with my hands and feet bound together, and I could only lift my head up to see the others ahead of me.

Other people were all tied the same as me, with their heads down, hands and feet together. I looked for Davey and Eddie. There they were on either side of me. They weren't alarmed;

they weren't fazed at all, like they had been in that position before. Motionless, they just sat looking down at the floor, as did everyone else.

"Help! Help me!" I began to scream but gave up knowing no one would hear me. The only light was what seemed to be a post in the front corner of wherever we were. I would call it a room, but to this day I didn't know where we were. The only thing I could remember was the position we were all situated in, similar to those who stood out before the fire, except this was different. We were forced into this place.

"Hello, all!" he said. I recognized his voice instantly. I tried to look up, but the pain in my neck was too severe to handle. "Here we are! Gathered together, like a family once again. Don't worry. Please, there is nothing to worry about!"

I looked to Davey and Eddie, but they didn't say a word.

"Now, we're going to try this again. You're all here because you failed to take your vows, or you failed to choose the right people to be around, and in turn, we're all here gathered as one," he said, hinting at me. I wondered right then and there why I had ever left Gabriella's sight. One second, I was fast asleep ready to head back home in the morning, and the next I was tied face down in a basement in some town I had never heard of.

He came into my line of sight just slightly, and when I craned my head, his entire wardrobe had been done over. There he was, sporting a black suit coat with an ever so slight tint of red. Flowers lined the entirety of it that could just barely be seen by the light coming off the fire. He was prancing around softly, like he was excited in his tone. His presence was disturbing. Long blond hair coaxed his shoulders, much thicker and more vibrant than the strands that wisped in the wind the night before. The tips of his pointed ears poked through, and his pale long hands clasped together as he spoke, like he was giving a presentation with every line he chose. He loved it. He loved the fear and attention we gave off, whether it was a crowd in attendance at their own will, or all of us tied to the floor of a basement room peering up at him.

Suddenly someone was making their way around the room, untying each person's hands from their feet as he went on. "I could leave you here if I wanted. One thousand years I could hold you here to think on what you've done, how you've been, who you could be. But I am as merciful as I am mighty, and for that, you'll try again. You all know what you have to do, where you have to be. And with that I'm off to keep saving the world!" he said, pulling a door open behind him and starting up a flight of stairs.

My hands were then cut free. With a clean slice my bindings fell apart to the floor. I was sore from being held for hours, and the pain in my head was only getting worse. As I stood to my feet, composing myself was hard, but I looked to Davey and Eddie who motioned me toward them before I could make out a word.

I followed them up the same flight of stairs. The essence in the room was the opposite of gleeful. Dozens of confused faces, people rubbing their ankles and wrists in pain, mumbling to those beside them. I still felt out of place, and I was. I didn't have a single clue why I was there or who these people even were.

As we got to the top of the steps, we came out into an old pub. The walls were dark wood, stale cigarette smoke lingered in the air, and live lanterns with fire dancing among them were nestled in every corner of the room. It was as if everyone in the bar knew what was going on. They didn't take a single look at us when we came up from the basement. I peered out the window and instantly knew where we were.

Just across the street was the motel that Gabriella was at. I started toward the door but was immediately halted by two men much larger and more intimidating than myself. They didn't say a single word, but their body language told me I wasn't leaving that place.

I started back toward the center of the room and spun around looking for a window. I was growing anxious and tired. I looked for any sign of an exit other than the windows at the front of the bar. The smoke was becoming too thick to handle, and as I started toward the back of the bar Davey called out with his back turned to me.

"There's no use, man. That's the exit. You're looking at it; they're standing at it. Just come sit down and have a drink," he said, sitting up at the bar with a glass already in his hand. Eddie was next to him standing with his back to the top, glaring at the floor before him.

"Man, I just don't get it. I was able to do my shit; it's your turn now. I mean, shit, the guy was blind and I still did it!" Eddie said, yelling at Davey.

"So, what did we do there earlier today? What is it that's honestly going on? You guys dragged me into this, you might as well give me an explanation," I said in a serious but calm tone so as to not piss them off.

The bartender looked to me for a drink, but I waived him off. I then instantly grabbed his shoulder in protest of my own action and motioned for a beer. I was craving it with the amount of anxiety that was swirling around in my head. There was a brief pause. Davey took a sip and then turned to me,

"You really have no idea where we are, do you?" he said to me.

I looked to him with wide eyes and a silent tone that suggested I was awaiting a further answer.

"Well, if you don't know where we are and what we're doing, then you obviously don't deserve to either. Just keep your head down, and if something happens, stay out of it," he replied.

His answer was much shorter than satisfactory. I thought of how to approach the question in a less demeaning way. I looked to Eddie, but he had already ordered his fourth shot and wasn't friendly in his gesturing, so I figured I'd just keep to myself.

"So, what now?" I asked.

As soon as I said that, a loud burst of lightning cracked through the sky, lighting up the night outside of us. The thunder rolled heavily following it, and then the pouring started. It was heavier than the night that I drove down here. So heavy it sounded like hail, close to bursting through the window. I looked around the bar; no one had jumped at the sound of the storm, just myself. Looking to the two, I tried to provoke a conversation, "Crazy weather you guys have out here," to which they both silently shunned my comment and looked back to their drinks.

Growing more anxious by the minute, I walked around pacing back and forth in the bar, checking the clock against the wall as it struck each minute. Seconds dragged on like sandbags across the mud, and the smell of cigarette smoke became much thicker the longer we stayed inside.

Once I finally stood in one spot I peered at the walls before me, stunned at the depictions I saw. Skeletons danced around a fire, hoisting spears high into the air. Old men and women barely clothed prancing around a forest. "LIMBO BAR, How Low Can *You* Go?" was hoisted over the backsplash of the bar itself. I take it that was the name of this place.

I made it a point to tell this to the officers once I escaped here and turned in these wicked and vile beings. They'd kidnapped me and were holding me against my will. My first plan was to escape, my second to tell everyone I knew about this wicked place and ask my grandfather why he hadn't warned me.

I grew upset with him, upset with my family. If they had just been honest with me as a child; had I just grown up to know that losing a family member was normal. Why would they hide something like this from me for so long and have me run off to such a wild land to search for my brother, or what was left of his legacy?

My anxiety was heightened, and with that I began to cry. I was in the corner of the room, and the lantern didn't extend this far. As I cried, I grew angrier and angrier at the people in my life who led me here. My anger was boiling inside me, and I felt the dark around me was swallowing me whole. The dark was heating my skin and my clothes, and my neck was burning before I finally stood up as someone swung open the front door to the bar. There he was again, as tall as he was before, as strong and menacing as he seemed prior. His newfound long blond hair was curled up in a bun, exposing his pointed ears. The teacher stood gazing at me, and then toward Davey and Eddie. He put his hand toward them both and motioned for them to follow.

At fault of my claustrophobia in that place, the anxiety of being forced to stay, I was almost happy that I got to maybe leave with them. My wishes were soon halted when the man sat at a round table at the other corner of the bar. Two men in suits stood above him on either side, as large as those by the door. His demeanor had changed. The man who stood at the head of the crowd in the woods the night before now sat like the head of a crime ring who was about to tell us our time was nearing an end.

Sitting across the table from him, I could feel the cold he resonated. The thick smokey air mixed with the chill of his words, delivering an all-too-dreadful tone. His sly and nice voice was turned in, and in its stead was a deep and ominous bundle of words that would scare away the evilest of human beings.

"Gentlemen, you have yet to come to peace with yourself. Therefore, I am yet to seal your deal. Davey, Eddie here has done his share of your promise. Am I to think less of your half of the decree?" he asked.

I still didn't have a single clue what was going on, but in context now knew it had something to do with the blind man. Out of pure fear I waited before asking any questions and was perplexed by the man and those who accompanied him.

"*Are you not to do what you said you would do?*" He now shouted, and simultaneously all the lanterns went out in the pub. The music halted. Those who were chatting now shared indistinct mumbles. I could only see the whites of his smile before us and the border of his eyes outside of where his pupils sat.

In a sly and sinister tone, he continued, "I know you will do what needs to be done. We will make sure of it, Davey."

"I know I will too. I was just trying to get Alec here away from it. I thought I'd—"

"You thought you'd what, Davey? Spare him from his lesson? Spare him of the one true thing he has to learn in this world—that nothing good comes from a perfect life?" he said, cutting Davey off.

"I just need to get back to my family. I haven't talked to them in days, and I just came out here to poke around, anyway," I said in a frail tone.

"Ahh but there you are wrong, Alec. No one comes out here just to poke around. You're not out here at your own will. Are you?" he asked.

If he was asking if that referred to the fact that I was tied to the basement floor an hour earlier, then no, but I knew such wasn't the case.

"I don't think I follow," I added.

"Alec, Davey, and Eddie. In due time, you'll all follow. You'll all do much more than follow."

With that, he stood from his place at the table and continued toward the door. The pub was still silent. Lights were being relit. I looked over through the window, and there she was. Off in the distance was Gabriella sitting up on the patio just as we did the night before. I was staring right at her, and her right back at me. Why didn't she come to help me?

If I could only just get up and through that one door, I could be back to her and escape this place. Just that one step. But it was impossible with those people in the way, and with that I looked at her until she stood to her feet, picked up her trash, and started back toward her room. She closed the door behind her, and simultaneously the two men at the door of the pub did the same. We were trapped there then, and I still didn't know what for.

Chapter 12

———

A little while longer we sat in the pub, looking at each other, drinking beers, talking about memories of things we never cared for and times we never wondered about. It was just a release, a solace in the chaos of whatever was going on. I think at that point I was still in shock. Telling stories about my father and family put my mind at ease.

One story that Davey told me of his father was particularly memorable, as it related to my father as well. He talked about this one certain thing his father always did to him after coming home from work. As a child he would hoist Davey into the air and blow on his bellybutton, then airplane him around the house until his mother forced them to stop.

And at the time it wasn't that which resonated with me, but the smell that Davey talked about that made me sad. He said his father's hands always left him smelling like engine oil and grease when he was done play fighting. His father smeared his clothes, and his mother would come in and yell at them both to go shower. My father was the same way, and I bet my brother would've been happy to hear that story from Davey as well, had he been there too.

I sighed in memory of how my father used to be more endearing when I was younger. The countless play times and nights out catching fireflies were swapped with showing me how to work on car engines and being worried about getting jobs done.

The pub was still darkly lit with a few passersby coming in and out. I felt as though we were the only people who weren't allowed to leave. Talking about my parents with the two made me worry about what they thought. I left very abruptly, and my parents already lost one of their sons. I felt bad about how worried they must have felt not hearing from me. When I got up to ask the bartender if there was a phone I could use, out swung the doors, and a cool rush of air made its way into the bar behind me.

I turned to see the teacher back again with his same group of men, motioning for us to follow him out to his vehicle. He owned a large black stretch limo, like he was a politician or something and we were about to make our way to a big event.

Leaving was nice, honestly; the humid and stuffed atmosphere of the pub was becoming too much to handle. As we got out to the car I thought to run in Gabriella's direction, away from the men. Out of fear that they had weapons on them or were much faster and stronger than me, I continued into the car and sat beside Davey and Eddie.

"You know, I used to be a very powerful and very beloved man," the teacher said, followed by a sarcastic laugh from

Davey. He smirked and looked to the window beside him. "Now I am an even more powerful and very hated man. Nevertheless, a better one for it as well!" he said with a grin so large it seemed animated.

And out of nowhere, I started, "You know, I came out here to find out whether my family's dark secret was all a lie, or whether my grandfather was just going senile when he said he had a house deep in the woods. At first, I admired this small town and what it didn't have to offer. One missed step and I'm all of a sudden sitting in a car with two guys I barely know and a crime lord who's probably going to kill us—"

Before I could finish my thought, he cut in, "Ahh, but Alec, you have yet to learn the truth. I know why you ventured to your great grandfather's house. I know why you held your brothers jacket so close to your heart."

"Wait, how do you—" I tried to interject.

"Alec, the rain isn't meant to meet the window of your car. The leaves aren't meant to crunch under your exact pair of feet. The dog wasn't born to die right under the bumper of your truck. Or was it? You see, life is a set of events, my son, but I have a specific gift. One that may help me to counter the events of one's life, repeat them to bring the true nature of the world out of each human, and sanctify who they really are. Look at young Eddie here, stealing from an old blind man with nothing, feeling the raw emotion pour from his heart as he takes away something that the man held near and dear. You think that was his first time doing this, Alec? I was merely copying his actions and having them displayed to prove to him and everybody else who he inevitably is!" he continued.

"But that isn't how the world is," I added. "You don't get to define people by their mistakes and wrongdoings. Who even are you? How the hell do you know about that dog? If you take a second of someone's life, even a year, and highlight that until the day they die, then obviously they can be nothing more than their problems. But what if you highlight the good they've done, the people they've loved—then what?" I exclaimed, trying to change his mind.

To no avail he began to chuckle in his uniquely sinister tone, something that still rings in my ears to this day. "Alec, my son, you will one day realize why I do what I do—how I help who I help. I give a home to the displaced, the ones who have no other realm in which to lie above the earth. I give a meaning to the damned, a resolution to their struggles. I change the quo that so defiantly shatters all characteristic unless it is confined and sound. I am righteous for the souls of the strong, absent minded in the face of the weak."

The man himself was so blinded by rage and anger that he resonated with those around him. He was picking on people who were so broken, who felt so failed by the world around them that they felt as though they were alone with nowhere to turn. Only then would it be time for him to swoop in and give them a chance at redemption, in a way that no one should seek to turn.

"So, what now?" I asked. "Am I going to die or something? It's not like you're just going to release me after this car ride. Where are you taking us?"

"Eddie, why don't you tell Alec who it was you robbed just moments before you came back to my lovely abode? Go on, son, tell him how good you did," he added.

Eddie was curling his fingers. Obviously uncomfortable, he sat in silence with his eyes wide. He was in distress, and finally after a long pause he said, "He was the same man I hurt once before. It is only in continuance that you solidify your substance in this place," he added as if he was reading a script.

"*What*?" I added. "Dude, I barely know you, but you've never sounded that weak and robotic like you just did. What are you talking about?"

"Don't you get it, son?" the teacher then said. "Eddie here was just working to solidify his place here. If we make a mistake once, we have the chance to be retrieved to the light, but if we do it again, we are whole in who we are and can accept our wrongdoing as nothing more than a piece of us forever."

I looked out the window; the rain had once again commenced. It was so loud and obtrusive that I had to raise my voice to be heard even with the windows rolled, and the teacher looked to me smirking, knowing that he could hear me but didn't care to listen. The further we ventured from the pub, the thicker the air got. The darker the forest became, the harder it was to comprehend. I felt in that moment like my consciousness was slipping. I thought to try the door next to me but didn't even have the strength to lift my hand.

I felt I was in a dream. I wanted to leap from the car and roll across the side of the road, run from them and never look back. Instead, my body became frail and frozen. In a dream-like state, I couldn't even move a muscle past my fingers. My mind was racing with ideas and plans, but my body was stagnant in response.

"Let's just get it over with!" Davey screamed, his first words since we got into the car.

"Ah, yes, my boy! That is what I'm talking about," the teacher replied. And with that the car came to a screeching halt. We were forced out by the men beside him, and blindfolds were slipped over our faces.

As we approached wherever we were going I felt the rain slipping right off me as if I were waterproof. Like tears down my cheek, each drop rode along my frame and ended on the ground below me. Even my clothes weren't penetrable to the droplets.

We were pushed through a passageway and the rain ceased, signaling that we had entered a room. When the blindfolds were taken off, shock overtook my entire body. I couldn't believe what was happening. Before me was a balcony that overlooked the entire structure we were situated on. A small box TV stood to my right, and a kitchenette to the other side. There were two sets of stairs on either side of the loft-style balcony overlooking the entirety of the house.

The teacher stood at the top of the stairs looking down on us. With his hands wide open he said, "Welcome, gentlemen! I think all but Eddie knows just exactly where we are! Don't you?" he continued.

I knew where we were, but everyone else? I was stunned. We had been brought back to my grandfather's old house. We were forcibly bent to our knees by the men. I didn't see the old man who lived here just one day before. Maybe he was out fishing. Maybe he'd be back just in time to save me from whatever was going on.

The teacher looked behind him and said, "Ah, yes, here it is! Davey, I have a present for you!"

There was no way. No way that any of this was actually happening. No way that anything I was seeing was true. I looked to Davey at my side, and his face told me I was wrong. He instantly began to cry as the man threw the jacket down off the loft before him.

"Put it on, son." He looked to me. "I suppose it should be a perfect fit!"

Chapter 13

———

I looked to Davey as he slipped it on, the same way I did, left arm following the right. Over one shoulder and connecting to the next like it was tailored to fit. Perfectly it sat high on each shoulder, heightening his frame and adding a brooding masculine tone to his stature.

"There's no way. How are you…? Who are you…?" I said to Davey. I was perplexed. I looked down and back up again. The teacher was staring down at us as if he expected the two of us to know what was going on. I still didn't find the old man. He was nowhere to be found. I started to pray that he would burst through the door and find some way to save us, some way to make sense of what was going on.

Nothing happened. Davey looked to me, and Eddie patted him on the back as they started back out the door. As the teacher started down the stairs, his footsteps each held the weight of stone. Like boulders pounding along each board, they made waves throughout the house as he approached me. I looked up at him. Still frozen from shock he asked, "What's the matter, boy? You act like you've never known your own brother before." And with that he brushed by me and through the door after them.

My parents hadn't lied to me. How would Davey be my brother? I never asked his age but there was no way he looked any older than me. On the other hand, though, how hadn't I guessed it? His name was Davey, my brother was allegedly David. Did he know I was his brother?

Even with all those questions circling around in my head, there were no familiar or friendly faces to answer them for me. I thought to run into the woods and then hitchhike to find a ride back to town. If I had just talked to my parents back at home all of it would've been fixed. I started for the door and took a hard left, only to bump into a man almost double my size, so tall that his chin was only visible when I looked up at it.

He grabbed my shoulders and pushed me toward the car. Another man aided him from my other side as I stumbled to keep up with their forced movements. We walked toward the car where I was ushered in to sit again across from the teacher, beside Davey and Eddie.

"I don't want any questions to be asked at this time. If a single person opens their mouth, it'll be the last word they ever speak. Understood?" the teacher said, looking at the three of us.

My shoulders were collapsing into my arms like they had suddenly dislocated. The adrenaline and fear and emotion were a mix of might that overtook my capacity to sit still. My foot was tapping so loudly that Davey at one point pushed his on top of mine, forcing it still. When he looked down into my eyes his stare was cold and hard. Was this my brother?

We continued driving for a short while. The music was eerie. Raspy old classical tunes with a foreign voice speaking a language I had never heard. It didn't sound like any modern language I could recall, maybe a dialect or something that very few people spoke, but the teacher was humming it like second nature. His dark and brooding voice took over the high-pitched singers' tones. Their singing together made for a disturbing rendition, given the circumstances.

At that point, it was the thickest air I had breathed in my entire stay in this town. To say my meeting with my brother was bittersweet would be a lie. I wasn't at all amused or happy to finally meet him.

When we finally arrived at our destination, I saw it. In big bold letters it stood out larger than it had any day before that I had seen it. The open sign on the outside of the gas station was more a warning than a welcome.

In the strangest hint of darkness that I had ever seen in my life, I looked up to see a sky so dark that red shone through its hinted tones. A milky fog hung in the air that would choke you had you not paid attention to each breath. Even my vision was impaired beyond this point, and other than what truly happened in the end, I don't remember much of what built up to then.

We got down from the car and continued into the shop. No music was playing, and the only lights were from torches lit by men and women lining the halls. All their eyes were closed as they stood firm as stone. As Davey entered, I could notice the angst in his stature. Although poised and strong, he shook his shoulders as if he wanted to build adrenaline, and I could see the weariness in his eyes as they widened and closed with each step closer.

I could hear someone struggling from above, calling out for help. We continued up into the attic of the shop, and there he was.

Dangling outside of the window, by the hands of two men, was the man who had asked us to take Davey with us to get him out of this place and away from his shop and this town. To make Davey understand a future beyond this place where he was stuck, beyond these people who he was involved with.

I was seated at the back of the room by one of the large men, frozen in fear. The attic was tight, and people stood all around holding drinks and wearing fine clothes, dressed as if this were an event, a spectacle. I felt the air choking me, surrounding my insides and flanking me as it drowned me in heat and discomfort.

Nothing was making sense. I started to smack my head in the hopes that I would wake up. That something would take over me and I would see my bedroom walls, brew a cup of coffee, and make my way for the balcony.

He looked to me, upside down, and instantly stopped his screams. "Alec. Don't worry. There's no way you could've known. No one gets it the first time. Even your parents didn't see it. No one can truly see it: evil. Evil is so hidden; so deeply hidden that we can't even see it in our own family." Before he could finish, the teacher interrupted.

"*Enough*! I will have no dissertation in the middle of my prophecy finally being taken to fruition. Davey, you are who you are because you understand your truth!" And with that he touched his fingertips to Davey's head.

I tried and tried to force myself out of the corner but to no avail. I was glued down as if I had been forced to stay. The teacher stepped back from Davey, and Eddie patted him on his shoulders as if to get him ready for what he was meant to do.

"Davey. You have no one but us. Your family, your friends, they all abandoned you. Your mother was pregnant with him," he said pointing to me. "They abandoned you because it got too much to handle. Davey, I will never abandon you. I have countless children, and still I will look after you like one of my own," he said.

Davey looked back at me, perplexed by what the teacher had said.

"He's... he's my *brother*?" he asked, tears starting to well in his eyes.

The rain outside had once again commenced. Daybreak was starting, but the sun wasn't a warm orange tinge; it was red, and it boiled in the sky, pushing rays so intrusive into the earth that I felt them through the walls of the room.

"Davey! It doesn't matter if he was your brother. He's nothing to you now! Why wouldn't he be here? If he really cared for you like I do, why wouldn't he be helping you right now? I just told you! Your family gave up on you because of him, Davey!" the teacher said, trying to convince him of his wishes.

The teacher's voice and prose were slipping. It's easier now to say and realize, but in that moment his vulnerability shone. He knew Davey had emotion for me, and he knew that he wanted to be back with my family and me. He was scared, and with that I tried, but even though I tried it wasn't enough.

"Davey. David. I don't know what to believe anymore. Mom and Dad, they miss you. They talk about you all the time. They—"

"He's lying, Davey! He's lying to you. Eighteen years they didn't think to look in your direction, and now you'll believe this man's words? Seal your fate. It's all you need to do, and you'll be fulfilled forever more!" the teacher continued in a tone that filled the room. The air was so thick I couldn't even breathe over it. His words wrapped around my head, each letter making its way into my ears in a slow and agonizing fashion.

I didn't know what to say. I didn't know how to reassure him. At the moment I was too young and too ignorant about where I was to even know there was a chance he would listen. I just slumped back into the seat and let the fear delve into me. I let the teacher's words petrify me and implode every inch of my body as I sighed in disbelief and just watched.

The man hanging in the window looked to me and smiled like he was okay with what was coming next. Like it had happened before.

Davey walked over to him, and without a second thought, there he went.

In the blink of an eye, he did exactly what my parents had told me.

He let him go, and there my uncle went.

Right before my eyes my own brother sealed his fate— renewed his solidarity with evil.

He looked the devil straight in the eyes and continued to walk in its direction. I couldn't feel anything.

He turned back to me. Tears were stuck in his eyes, hugging at their last wit to stay locked to his lashes, but they fell beyond his cheeks and slammed against the floor, loud enough for us all to hear it over the silence of the room.

And the teacher. There he sat, looming over him—taller and stronger than ever before—as if he fed off the energy Davey had just committed to him. This was a figure, a figure that would haunt me for the rest of my life. That black lifeless mass that swung above my brother and swept him into his grasp. He just sat there mocking me as he walked behind him.

Davey didn't even look to me before leaving the room. His gaze was targeted to the floor below him. Although he knew what he had done wrong, he still did it. He knew what was going to happen, and he still went through with it.

I blamed myself. I knew what would happen, and I didn't try to stop him.

Eddie took him by the arm and walked him out the door, followed by the teacher and his henchmen close behind. In time I sat frozen, looking out the window from where my uncle just fell. I didn't have the heart to look over the window—I wouldn't.

Instead, I just stayed, looking at the floor below me.

There he left. In one instant, a stranger. In the next, he was the one person I was looking to find, but he wasn't himself. Or was he?

The air cleared the further they got away from me. My breath ceased to be hindered by the air, and the smoke and red clouds were swapped with a cold calming rain. It wasn't hail, it wasn't strong, and it didn't slap against the walls of the room around me.

Instead, it fell like mist. It dribbled down to the earth as softly as snow. Each drop was like a solemn and slow tear dusting off the face of the sky.

And then she arrived. From behind me she hugged me, and her embrace was as warm as fur, smooth as silk. Her voice, as little as I had heard it, was distinctively known to me.

"It's done now, Alec. You mustn't think about it anymore," Gabriella said in a soft and much more mature voice.

She was the same, but her words were swapped with a sophistication, a knowledge that was more prevalent than before.

She spoke to me with nothing but wisdom and ushered me out to her car one last time. I wept slowly and deeply. I had never expected to be so close yet so far separated from my brother.

I looked around the lot and didn't see any of them. Not my brother, not the teacher, not even my uncle or any of the men who accompanied them. The sign at the front of the shop was now dark, not a single bulb illuminated.

"Alec. The world is meant to work in the way that it does. Trust me, there will be other times. You don't have to understand now; no one gets it the first time. One day, though, one day you'll see us again," she said.

"*No!* That teacher—or whatever the hell they call him! He said it himself! He's stuck here forever. I don't even know where here is, and I don't know what to do. Take me back to the bar! Take me back there now!" I demanded. In that moment I was acting out of shock. "How could he have been that stupid to think that stranger, that... that whatever the fuck it was had anything to offer him!" I shouted as Gabriella kept her calm and looked to me.

"Alec, I have to tell you something now. I'm going to let you go. I have to let you go," she said.

I was confused and sat motionless as she kept saying, "I have to let you go."

"I have to let you go. You failed. It's not your fault. But I have to let you go."

Chapter 14

———

"She did let me go. She did return me to where I came. I don't remember the rest of the ride home or continuing to my house, because none of it happened. As I sat there staring at the dashboard my brain started to collapse. My joints began to crack, and my head started to feel weary and heavy.

"My eyes shut with the force of a million hands pulling them down against me. My body slumped into the chair, and I fell into a dream, or actually the exact opposite. I awoke with a pounding in my head. I couldn't see at first, as my eyes felt as they had been shut for ages."

"And then what? I mean... did you just wake up? It was all a dream, or what?" Aaron asked on the other side of the table at Sully's.

I felt bad for him. Almost three decades since the incident and I hadn't even thought to reach out to him. Then again, I had lost most of my connection to my entire family at that. Once my father and mother passed away, I just sank into that town as best I could.

I continued to explain to him how it all happened. "I don't remember much except for when I finally came to."

. . .

"Honey! Honey, I think he's awake!" I had heard this voice since the day I was born. Words spoken in a familiar tone and sounds so recognizable they could only be from my own mother's mouth.

I still couldn't see by this point. The pain in my head was throbbing almost to a synchronous beat. I tried to move up to my arms to sit but they quickly pushed me back down as if to tell me it wasn't a good idea. When my eyes finally opened fully, I looked around and noticed the room around me.

When the hearing commenced, I heard the *beep, beep, beep* of the machines hooked to my arm. The room was pristine and white, each thing meticulously placed, not a single item out of place. No old board games lying around or trash hanging out of the wastebaskets. This was a beautiful place, one of healing, but also one of final goodbyes.

In that moment—when I felt the way I did just as I had every other day of my life when I awoke next to my balcony watching the sun spill through my window—I felt that maybe I was just asleep. Maybe I was just asleep, and I was having a dream so vivid and so real that the world seemed to bend around me in mysterious ways.

Maybe I was having a dream just as Gabriella had explained to me. A dream so vivid and real but so horrifying that it would be safer to just move from it and not try to explore deeper than what it presented to me.

My mother began to cry and—as my eyes fully opened—so did my father, who burst out the door of the room screaming for a doctor to come in. When they returned there was a doctor and two nurses who followed. They stood on either side of him as he started reading from a clipboard.

"Hello, Alec. How are you feeling?" he said in a soft and welcoming tone.

"I—I'm fine. I just don't understand fully what's going on," I replied. The first words came out dry and tough as they left my mouth. I could barely make out the words I thought to say.

"Well, Alec, I'm going to take this slow because you did just wake up, but we have to tell you what happened for your own good. You were in an accident. While you were driving, you collided with a tree across from a motel about an hour or so from your house. Do you remember that happening, Alec?" he spoke.

I started to freak out, not just emotionally but physically. My body tweaked and shivered as he unraveled the truth of the previous days. I was looking around the room in every which way thinking how this was possible. I was at the motel. I was at a motel, but I didn't get into an accident.

"My truck broke down. A woman was there! She helped me; she gave me a ride to my grandfather's house. I wasn't in an accident, I was there. I was fine!" I replied in a sharp tone to deny what he had told me.

In all my panic I hadn't even seen him there, but I looked out of the corner of my eye. My grandfather was beside the bed curling his hat in his hands. He looked sorrowful, like he regretted sending me in that direction. If what they had said was true, I'm sure he blamed himself.

"Alec, listen. I know it may not seem real right now, but you were in a coma now for about three days. I can't say it's normal, but I have seen patients return to the scene of their accidents whilst in a comatose state. It's possible you were imagining where you were while you were inside," he continued.

I looked to my parents. "No! I saw him. I saw both of them. I saw David's jacket. I saw the house. I saw him get dropped out of the window!" I broke down crying. My mother in turn started to weep as well. They all couldn't believe the things I said.

Even the doctor was confused as to how vivid and clear my memories of that time were. I was stuck in that hospital for only three more days thereafter, and in that time, I racked my brain as to how it was possible. How all of what I experienced was only but a dream.

"Everything was so real," I whispered under my breath, looking at my hands and feet before me. "The rain, the rain I felt, it was pressed against my skin. The air was cold. All of it was so real," I continued.

The doctor continued to explain to me that none of these feelings were abnormal; they were just as common as other patients who had experienced these states, and so they were written off as no more than shock. "Well, Alec, we've had other patients talk about characteristics of their state being dependent on their surrounding outside here in the room. Rain, for example. It's quite possible that your parents crying by your side was translated into weather patterns or things you experienced while in that state," he went on.

The motel—the first night I got there; right after I had passed there was a storm. It was so rainy, and the drops were falling so hard I had to stop, but then Gabriella said she hadn't noticed any rain.

Throughout the next few nights in that hospital, I continued to have a dark and sinister feeling that I couldn't put my finger on. Every memory of that place was like a failure. Every second spent there in hindsight seemed like I could've done something better. I could've made David more understanding of something that even I didn't know about.

The first night after I left, I begged for my parents to stay by my side. I apologized countless times for leaving them, but in reality, once I was awake the one thing I wanted more than anything was to go back.

I had planned my departure from the time I left the hospital to the second I could get my hands on another car.

. . .

"Well… so what did you do next? I mean, I didn't even know where you were or what happened to you. None of us did. I didn't even see you at your parents' funeral," Aaron continued.

I was there, truthfully, just off in the distance. After what I had done to David, and how I failed him, I couldn't really do much of anything with my family.

All throughout my life the memories continued to creep into my nights. I would go a year almost without a single episode but would be shaken to my core one night by a vivid memory of what happened, and I would see the teacher's sharp and colossal shoulders and black cloak swarming around rooms that were more common like my house or the place I worked.

I never married because I struggled with the idea of companionship, with the responsibility of another person's life. I blamed myself for what happened to David and the ultimate decision he made, even though I didn't truly know it was him. All it took was those words Gabriella said, "You failed. I can't tell you why, but you failed."

"One day, as I planned, I went back to find my grandfather's old house. It was the day of his funeral, two years after the events of the coma. We buried him with my grandmother, all went our separate ways, and I couldn't sleep that night thinking of what his house looked like in real life. I thought of the stew the old man made me, same as the one he had. I thought of standing up on that balcony, pulling the key from the belly of that frog, and so I leapt up and drove in the middle of the morning. Didn't tell my parents, not even you, and I am sorry about that. Truly, Aaron, I am.

"When I arrived, daybreak was just commencing. It was in the same place as it had been before, and the weirdest part was that on the way, there was a motel, there was a gas station, even an old pub that stood before the motel just like the one I had seen in the dream.

"Instead of large signs illuminating the roads and people stumbling out of the bar, it was a deserted town, forgotten by everyone, dead to the world. When I finally reached the house, it was nothing of its original self. The foundation had sunk into the floor of the earth. The roof had caved in on itself after so many years. It saddened me to see my grandfather and his father's work this broken and small, so different than I had seen it in my dream.

"In that moment I believed what the doctor said. Dreams have meanings sometimes no more interesting than what we think about on that day or in that moment. I tried the door and walked into the house to find nothing. It was completely gutted; there was no staircase that led up to a balcony that overlooked the entirety of the house. Instead, there was just a pile of wood, sunken, broken, reeking of mold, years of rain and decay.

"The smell wasn't of smoke; the air wasn't thick. It was clear, and I had no problem being there. The solace and silence of the cabin was almost beautiful in its broken state. I stood back at the door and peered once again over my shoulder at the interior, thinking of the events that occurred, and with that I started back to the motel.

"When I arrived, there wasn't a young woman sitting up watching a television. There were no people anywhere in sight. As dreary as the place was in my dream, it wasn't anything compared to the lifeless spectacle I was in the second time I arrived. I walked back out and on to the rooftop where her and I sat, and as the sun was still rising, I sat in the same spot as we had when she told me of her dream. I looked out at the pub across the street, realizing that she could see me that day when I was looking back up at her, trapped in there.

"I got up and walked to her room, and to my surprise there wasn't anything I had expected to see. The only things there were signs. They alluded to a life not lived—to a life not fully had by a girl who deserved more. A crib sat in the corner of the room, with a basket small enough to seat a newborn child. From the other side of the room there were large suitcases, half emptied with swimsuits and various other clothing items lining the floors.

"Across the room at the desk, there was a news clipping. It was alone, torn out of a paper from years ago, old and dusty but still legible.

"Freak Accident Takes the Life of Newborn Gabriella Alvarez."

"People always ask why terrible things happen to innocent people. Why sickness, death, and war come to those who least deserve it. They swear at God and propel anger for the things that happen to people across the world. Gabriella didn't deserve to die so young, but just as her dream had told, she was in the end, held in the embrace so tight and so overbearing that it took away all her fear of the unknown."

"Alec. I'm sorry. I'm sorry you didn't find what you were looking for—"

"Well, that's the thing, Aaron. I hadn't been able to let go of the fact that I didn't find what I wanted. I didn't believe that my grandfather would've sent me in the direction of nothing; he had to know something. I started on the cabin. That year, and all the years that followed, I started rebuilding the cabin to its original glory," I continued, Aaron's eyes starting to widen.

"I got a job in the town next over from that place—nothing special. I worked trades all over town, learning how to build, plumbing, all the stuff I'd need to apply it to the cabin and motel. It took years and years, but now that I'm back I can say I finally did it. At least as close to what it seemed, really. The motel is back to its original glory, and the cabin looks just like it did when I was there years ago. The balcony overlooking the open concept; everything in its original place," I said.

I continued to explain to him. On and on the words flooded out of my mouth, and I realized I sounded like a mad man. How I had recreated a dream so vivid, so recognizable that I might be able to get another chance at what I was looking to solve.

"I would sit up all night. Every day after work I would wait. I would wait for the footsteps of the leaves crunching around the woods. Maybe Davey and Eddie would push through the door and tell me to come with them. Maybe Gabriella would honk from outside the motel, motioning for me to come with her again. Every day and night I hoped for it. And there's still hope… I know it," I said, breaking down in tears in front of Aaron.

"Alec… come on, man. You can't throw away your whole life because of a dream. Dude, look at you. You look like you haven't showered in weeks, and you've been up for days. You showed up in this biker jacket like you're part of some damn gang, and your hair is so long it's getting on your plate. Man, I don't know what to say... I'm worried about you, dude," he continued.

"You're not wrong—far from it. I spent every waking second of my life regretting the fact that I didn't do what I should've. I cursed my father and mother for being able to go on with their lives—to live and have more kids and a family and do every little thing to push the memory of David out of their heads. It made me sick. I wouldn't be like that! I can't!" I shouted over the table.

"But, Alec. Have they come back yet? Have Davey and Eddie come to the cabin? Has Gabriella pulled up to see you? Has the teacher presented himself in front of you? Did anything happen outside of the dream that happened while you were in there? I mean, you said it yourself, Gabriella Alvarez was a newborn when she died," he said.

He wouldn't understand. He couldn't. I didn't blame him, though. He didn't go through what I did—didn't see the things I saw.

I was just carrying it all. I was just holding on to this damn load I couldn't shake. There it was: It had flooded over, and now it was seeping through my floors for all the world to see. I looked like a crazy old half-wit who gave half his life searching for answers that weren't there. I don't even remember what my motivation was anymore, just the fact that I had to see them again. I had to make sense of how I failed.

Whether it's out in the world in front of us or it's inside our heads—we all have things we carry. Whether we make peace with it or not, we will go on making it seem like our lives are normal. Like the people we hurt are healed. Like the experiences we had didn't shape us. Maybe there is a chance to change, or maybe there isn't. For a whole lot of us, though, I guess we never find out whether that's true.

Chapter 15

———

Dies Iudicci, Yawm ad-Din, Judgment Day. Another forty years went by, and I hadn't listened to anything Aaron told me to do. I continued to build. I continued to see what I could make of that town—how much I could recreate. Even the bar was almost done in the exact same way as I remembered it. If it wasn't for that damn fall, I would've still been out there working.

Beep... beep... beep. The clicks began to grow further apart the longer I sat in that room. After almost a week, I could feel the distance between each beep. I had memorized their place, one after another leading me to my demise.

I know my nurse just thought of me as another crazy individual in her care. She could hear me whispering about the teacher and Gabriella and how I knew I'd die and meet them once again.

I knew there were people who lined these halls with different disorders, and there was no shortage of stories within these walls. The amount of baggage, the amount of flooding this hospital felt from all the years of combined life and regret and mistakes, was so apparent. It was as amazing as it was depressing.

I'm eighty-eight now, and I could've still kept kicking. I could've still woken up every morning, making that same fish stew, walking those same streets, rebuilding that same past. I had so much more to build, so much more to experience before sitting in this hospital room and drawing my last breath.

From the height of the hospital I could see the town I had worked on for so many years. I felt like from that perspective that I was the only one with that last and final view. I saw the shop sign once more, so bright you wouldn't miss it from a mile away. And behind the shop, ever so slightly, I could see lights starting to pop up. One by one they made their way right to left, almost in a pattern, until one shone brighter than the rest burning high and hot into the sky. They were starting; they were rebelling. The rebellion was so loud and so bright that it could be seen all the way into the stars.

With that I knew where I was going. With that I knew I could let go.

It entranced me. I felt a light. I didn't just see it, but I felt it. The way it intruded my eyes and burnt my ears. The way it heated my cheeks and tightened my throat. It was painful but numb, a foreign feeling but a natural consciousness.

I almost felt myself sink into the back of my body, the top corner of my head remaining as it was, lying there on the bed. I almost felt a shaking. I almost heard the nurse screaming my name. I almost heard her whisper in my ear, "Goodbye, sir." I only felt nothing. I only felt the space created and the void unfilled. I only felt myself slip away.

I only felt the sun spilling through the window onto me. The light filled up the room and my head and the holes inside of me. I was hollow, expanded, and filled with light. I couldn't see myself, but I could swear I was dispersing, disintegrating into the open air. The sensation was better than all I had ever felt before. That was the most peculiar part.

. . .

As I finally came back to my senses, or so I thought, the air had begun to feel crisp around me. The wind was thick as it barreled against my skin, the clouds covered the sun in the sky, and I could now easily get up to my feet. I was thin and full of energy. I pressed my hands to my face and didn't feel any beard. No hair was falling down the sides of my head. My joints didn't ache; I could run, jump, yell, even hit things with a force I hadn't felt in sixty years. I looked before me only to see a forest, so thick and dense I couldn't make sense of any of it.

I was aware I had just died, but this wasn't what I expected to happen as I made my entrance to the afterlife. The air wasn't foreign; the smells were close to home, something I could easily identify. As I started to walk forward, I was careful not to twist my ankles on the branches below me, but I continued on until I came to a small clearing in the woods.

I was stunned to find a familiar structure, all too close to the one I had just been in hours before. Before me stood the cabin—the real cabin, and I could feel the difference truly. The actual one I hadn't seen in over fifty years since that dream I had. This wasn't the structure I recreated. The frog statue sat by the front door. The grass was perfectly maintained and freshly cut from the scent of it. Birds chirped. The air was calm and relaxing. I didn't have a single complaint.

I sprung up the steps and burst through the front door, falling to my knees as I entered. I couldn't believe my eyes. Years had passed, and I longed for this moment—longed for the opportunity to all be together in a place like this.

My mother and father, who had passed many years prior, my grandparents, they all sat before me in the small living room of this place. I couldn't believe my eyes. I had made it to heaven and my whole family was there with me.

As I embraced my parents and my grandparents, we all wept together sitting and sharing stories. I told them of the final years of my life they had missed and of my recollection of this place as much more than what it seemed to be. My parents reassured me that I was never crazy, that they had never doubted that I came here when I was in the hospital. Before I could tell them any more, the front door swung open.

In came a man sporting long old overalls, one clip unhooked with a line of fish hanging over his shoulder from his back to his belly. The man who took me in. The man who made me that stew, that same familiar stew I knew and loved.

"Alec. Go give your great grandfather a hug," my mother motioned me toward him.

"Alec, son. Forget about hugs. Let's take a ride, you and I." He beckoned as I instantly arose to my feet and followed him out the door.

As we got into his truck, the air began to thicken around me. I looked back one last time as my family all stood on the porch. Their gaze wasn't soft and complete anymore—it was worrisome. My father sat in the rocking chair looking to the floor.

And then I remembered. Where was David? He wasn't in the house with them. They hadn't even brought him up. I thought to ask, but it was like he read my mind instantly.

"Alec, what I told you many years ago was never a lie. Your brother was already dead when he came to me, and so was I. As you could guess, I've been dead for many moons. Your brother got into the same accident you did when he was on his way to the house, and for the same reason," he said.

"But if you've been here, what about your wife? My great grandmother, where is she? Why wasn't she there when I met you?" I asked.

"Well, son. Many years ago, a man tried playing God. He tried bringing someone back instead of just relying on God's wishes, and his eternal punishment is so..." he said, referring to the story he had told me years ago. "This, though, isn't what I wanted to speak to you about. It isn't the point. Did you even think of your brother David when you came back to this place?" he asked.

He was right. I was so caught up in seeing my family and my parents, I forgot that David wasn't with us. That he couldn't be.

"But I know where he is, and I thought there was no going back?" I asked.

"Our God is a very merciful one, Alec. Mistakes leave room for growth, room for rearranging the past. To make sense of your future, you have to make right of the past, however many times it may take. Look to the road before us; look to your left," he motioned.

A young boy was running from a store front, a bag of food and cash spilling out with each step he took. He looked afraid, miserable, and so many people were chasing him. We kept driving, and then on my right the same boy, the exact same one, stood in the middle of a field flying a kite with friends running around him. He was happy. His face shone a smile so bright that no one could tamper his spirits.

And then we kept driving. Out of the corner of my eye I saw a young boy sitting with a knife, his head in his hands. The man slowed down beside him, and he lifted his head. It was Eddie. He appeared much younger than before. As we kept driving, we came up to a house on the right side of the road. There was Eddie again, much older, holding sports equipment, leaving the house with a man's hand slumped over his shoulder. They looked happy, connected, like a family.

As we continued driving, we saw countless young boys and girls. On one side they were scared, alone, wallowing in the sorrow of their wrongdoing, and on the other they were surrounded by love and joy and happiness.

"Alec. There is a life we may have lived, and a life we can still attain. And in the middle, right there in the center where we are right now. There's a tale in between. You have control of this tale. You can help him to escape this if you wish. You didn't know before, but you know now," and as he said that we slowed to the left.

There he was. Davey was walking with a few other men. His face was hardened and cold, menacing at the very least.

"I know what to do. I've been here before, and even you know what happens next. However many times it may take, you said. Well, it should only be one more, because I won't let you all down again," I added.

"Alec. Life doesn't allow you to do the same things over again. The same goes for this place. Yes, you know what you have to do for Davey. But the path may not be as easy as it once was. Just because you spent decades rebuilding something you went through doesn't mean the exact same thing is going to present itself in front of you. That is why we tell you to let go of what you can no longer control."

The air grew thicker as it once did before, but I wasn't afraid. He couldn't be right. Gabriella would help me. I'd go to her first and see if she could give me that ride. Then we'd devise a plan from there. But things would end differently for us. I knew it.

"And this is where we stop, son. You can't see what's up on the right as you haven't experienced it yet. You haven't earned that side of the tale, but once you do, I'll be waiting. We all will. Come down from the truck now," he said, and with that he pulled to the right and I got out without a single thought.

I stepped out to a familiar sight. Goosebumps lined my arms as I shut the door behind me and stared at the massive motel ahead of me. There she was, outside cleaning her car, the same car I had left years ago.

"Gabriella!" I yelled to her to try and get her attention. She looked to me as confused as she was worried and walked in the other direction. I approached her faster as she ran around the corner, and with that I realized she had no idea who I was.

I started down the road until I came up on the gas station and again could not believe my eyes. Out of the shop came David, like he had transported from where I last saw him. My uncle was following behind him. I couldn't make sense of any of it. He had died right before my eyes when David chose to drop him. How was he walking with him as if nothing ever happened?

I heard her voice behind me. "Why did you yell my name? Who are you?" she said.

"Gabriella, it's me! It's Alec. I haven't seen you in years. Remember? You had to let me go. You had to let me go, and now I'm back! But David and my uncle, why are they... why is he still alive?" I asked.

She stared at me, still confused but with a look that told me she hadn't forgotten me, either. The air began to tighten around me. Clouds began darkening the sky, and a voice so naturally known to me made its presence. A voice with words that wrapped around my head, each letter landing directly behind my ears. Even if they weren't spoken to me, I know they were able to land on my ears as if they were. "She can't act like she remembers you, boy. That would ruin the purpose now, wouldn't it?"

It was him. It was the voice that had haunted me for years. Sleepless nights imagining his dark and brooding stature darting around me like he owned my head.

Gabriella turned and darted back toward the motel. My uncle and David got into their car and drove right by me without noticing me, as if we had never met. As I watched them drive by, I looked up to the edge of the forest. It was lined by people standing side by side. Perfectly synchronous, they stood like statues, hoisting torches and staring right through me.

I felt his presence stronger than anything in the world at that moment. It was like he grew from my energy. With a voice so prevalent and words that wrapped around my head as they spoke, he whispered into my ear.

"How about another try, boy?"

Acknowledgments

———

Firstly, I'd like to thank my family. My parents, Khalil and Lauren, and my sisters, Zayna, Ranya, and Leena, for always being there for me during this process and every other hurdle I face in life. Living in a home that encouraged my creativity and supported my thinking only furthered the success of this book. My mother has always pushed me to develop my writing and act on my passion for the art, whether I felt like I had enough time for it or not.

I'd also like to thank my fiancée, Nesrin, for being the ground that I walk on. Without her constant motivation and listening to my crazy story ideas, I wouldn't have been able to pursue a task this cumbersome while working and going to school full-time. My best friends, Chris, Riley, and Liam, have been there for me since the beginning and will continue to far past the publication of this book.

Professor Deborah Finch was the person who introduced me to this program, and without her guidance and constant mentorship week after week, I wouldn't have had the confidence to take on this piece and all that came with it. I thank her for believing this was something I could do and for staying by my side and seeing it through until the end.

Thank you to the Francis W. Parker Charter Essential School where I originally wrote my first draft. Debbie, my advisor; Christine, my first editor; and many more names that did more than they needed to give me the confidence that I could do this from the very beginning.

Special thank you to Georgia Tomao for helping me with my cover design inspirations. Without her artistic talents I wouldn't have been able to get my ideas out to the cover design team for an absolutely beautiful rendition of her cover mock-ups.

Lastly, a huge thank you to New Degree Press for giving me this opportunity from the start. Eric Koester, Brian Bies, Elissa Graeser, Jordana Megonigal, Katherine Mazoyer, and all those who I met along the way who pushed me forward and mentored me constantly.

Due to all of you, the words between these pages exist and were able to come to fruition. I am forever indebted to your efforts to make this piece a reality, and your contributions truly helped to make my dream come true.

I would also like to recognize all those who supported me through my campaign efforts. Due to the names listed below, this dream became a reality:

Khalil Basma, Lauren Basma, Zayna Basma, Ranya Basma, John Bresnahan, Chase Murphy, Deborah Finch, Amber

Fulmer, Brian Anderson, Samantha Kane, Sarah Pierce, Manny de Souza, Hayley Sheriff, Rayan Manoun, Mariam Abess, Holly Lalos, Timothy Manchester, Cathy Jaffee, Samantha Murphy, Sandra Murphy, Riley Murphy, Kassie Breest, Jill Harvey-Tesak, Eric Koester, Georgia Tomao, Tyler Sweeney, Kate Vizen, Mona Blanchard, Kristin McKenney, Alana Beaudreault, Cheri McDonald, Kimberly Noe, Pamela Reeves, Nicholle Reeves, Ava McDonald, William Noonan, Chris Smith, Anam Chaudhary, Margaret Kidder, Connor Begun, Debra Joy, Abigail Anderson, Yeaharne Hout, Lucas DeLisle, Kim Merriman, Molly Masciarelli, Mike Lanney, Felix Jordan, Brian Morin, Gretchen Cutter, Paul Boudreau, Kylee Donelle, Deborah Osofsky, Teri Cataldo, Nan Heighton, Sarah Devaney O'neil, Jill Manuel, Anita Reiser, William Thibodeau, Sharon Regonini, Jennifer Gendron, Zyann Sharkah, Autumn Tomao, Natalie Carroll, Isabel Doonan, Kevin Morin, Colman Richards, Spencer Lee, Colin DeLisle, Johanna Anziani, and Joe Ward.